VET ON VACATION

A Star Original

'Tango's a good dog. Been winning a lot of races for us. But you put 'im in a trap alongside a bitch and he loses every time. Holding back, he is; you can see it plain as daylight.'

I said nothing. Ernie had used one of the standard methods of seeking a free consultation. I'd fallen for it all too often . . .

Ernie patted his greyhound's rump. 'Well . . . I mean . . . I don't like to say it, but it i'n't natural, a dog what can't abide bitches. It i'n't nice, is it? Can't you give 'im a pill or something like they showed on TV? Sex-hormones or something?'

Also by Alex Duncan in *Star*

IT'S A VET'S LIFE
THE VET HAS NINE LIVES
VETS IN THE BELFRY
VETS IN CONGRESS
VET AMONG THE PIGEONS
VET IN A STATE
VET'S CHOICE
VET IN THE MANGER

VET ON VACATION

Alex Duncan

A STAR BOOK

published by
the Paperback Division of
W. H. ALLEN & Co. Ltd

A Star Book
Published in 1979
by the Paperback Division of
W. H. Allen & Co. Ltd
A Howard and Wyndham Company
44 Hill Street, London W1X 8LB

Printed in Great Britain by
Hunt Barnard Printing Ltd, Aylesbury, Bucks

ISBN 0 352 30357 3

One

'What's that? Michael! Listen!'

I jerked awake and almost fell out of the narrow top bunk. It took a few seconds to orientate myself. No, I was not on a ship. I was spending the first night of our summer holidays at Curate's Cottage, our own country home. And my wife and I were sleeping in a two-tier bunk-bed for practical reasons best known to her. With the builders about to start work on making our rural slum habitable Julia had foreseen that we'd have to keep moving our sleeping quarters; hence her bargain-buy of bunks, held together with a few butterfly screws, which could be assembled or dismantled in minutes.

Julia had lit the candle beside her bed. 'Didn't you hear it?'

'What?'

'It sounded like an earthquake.'

'In the south of England? Don't be silly, love.'

'I read somewhere that you hear an earthquake before it hits.'

'Julia, go to sleep.' Just then I too heard it; a deep rumbling followed by a crash like breaking glass. It had come from the direction of the unkempt land behind the vicarage and our cottage. Simpkins's pit, that's what the Craftly people called it. Long before we'd got to know the village Simpkins's father had worked it as a sand-pit, but the son – more keen on his profitable hardware and farm machinery shop – had abandoned the pit to the brambles and sycamore seedlings.

'It's coming nearer,' worried Julia. 'What could it be?'

'A lorry or a tractor.'

'At this time of night? Besides, there's no road.'

'I'll take a look in the morning.'

'That's when Mr Cobbler's coming.'

'Who?'

'The builder, Michael.'

'Well, I'm not getting up now.'

'I suppose it might have been something in the sky . . . breaking the sound barrier.'

Extraordinary girl, my Julia; so practical in some ways, so childish in others. Sound barriers and earthquakes indeed! Too much imagination, that was her trouble. And our eleven-year-old son, Mike, was taking after her . . . always dreaming up ways of breeding pests and parasites in the course of his zoology experiments. Full of ideas, most of them ingenious but trying for his parents. At least Andrew, our younger boy, was easy; stolid, like me.

The boys would have a great time at Craftly. With its friendly farmers, the Arab children at the Manor House and the new theatre, the village had become their magic place. The boys' pleasure, when I'd told them that Curate's Cottage was ours, had removed the last of my misgivings about buying it.

True, the place smelled damp, the electrics were a fire-hazard, the grit and worms that came out of the water-taps unsavoury – to say the least. Nor did we like the fact that the old-fashioned tank of the loo was screwed to a plank which was nailed right across the bathroom window, so that users were in danger of being charged with indecent exposure. On the other hand – as Julia had ponted out – the seat of the loo wasn't made of flimsy plastic but of fine solid oak. The oak of the inside beams and the rafters was equally impressive. Generations of woodworm and deathwatch beetle, plus damp and dry rot, hadn't succeeded in gnawing enough of the wood to make the structure unsafe.

Without admitting as much to Julia I agreed with her that it would all *come right in the end.* Her imagination and the work of decent country builders would surely turn Curate's Cottage into a gem.

I was drifting back to sleep. Nothing like fresh air; rose-scented too. The Albertina, which covered the whole wall under our windows, was in full bloom . . . looking a treat, though probably concealing ominous cracks in the old flint wall. I wasn't going to worry about it now. At eleven and a half thousand the cottage had been cheap, whatever state it was in. Julia, with the help of Clive Astley-Appledore, wouldn't overlook any defect.

Clive was a man of many parts; land-owning native of Craftly, estate agent and architect. Because we'd bought Curate's Cottage through his firm, and because he'd given us a reasonable deal, Julia had felt that we should employ him as our architect. Living in London we'd needed a local man to have our alteration-plans passed by the Council, to get builders' estimates and supervise the actual work.

Clive, slowly but surely, had done the necessary and come to the point where the builders could start. I had no reason to doubt Clive's efficiency, except Julia's confidence in him and the fact that she'd agreed to Clive's choice of builder – Cobbler & Sons Ltd – without a written estimate. Julia had assured me that country people didn't worry about such little details.

Real country builders were craftsmen and members of their traditional community. They'd expect the customer to take their word for it that the job would be properly done for the agreed payment. Clive had given Julia the fixed-estimate figure over the phone, she had jotted it down, and that was good enough for her. Besides Mr Cobbler had mentioned to Clive that he'd confirm the estimate in writing when his secretary got back from her holiday on the Costa Brava.

Curate's Cottage was the first house we'd owned. Julia would certainly enjoy resurrecting this ancient place. I listened to her quiet breathing in the bunk below. This time she didn't hear the approaching rumble of whatever the night-prowler was, nor too the crash of whatever was being destroyed.

If Old Harry of Yellow Streak hadn't bounded in we'd have overslept. London or country, our black and white mongrel wasn't going to have his routine interfered with, and a part of his routine was his ecstatic good-mornings.

Undeterred by our awkward bunks he greeted us with his high-pitched chatter, leaping on his hindlegs until he'd found a hand to pull down and lick. Not the most hygienic way of starting the day, but one didn't have the heart to rebuff Streaky. On the rare occasions when we'd left him in London we'd missed his performance – the daily thanksgiving for rediscovering his family. The sight of his slim head with the large eyes, one black and one white fluffy ear, made even me forget the infections which animals can pass on to man.

Julia got up and ran downstairs. I stretched until I stubbed my toes on the bottom rail of the bunk. Outside, a lark's song was rising into the clear sky. The sunshine flooding the low-ceilinged room reminded me of my childhood, of those richly golden mornings which now seemed unique. *A memory of ancient sunlight* someone had called it. Perhaps it could be recaptured, here, in the old cottage in Craftly. The smell of coffee mixed with paraffin and the children's voices made me climb out of the bunk.

Julia had made the kitchen quite attractive. The slatted

garden table she'd found in the shed was covered with a red gingham cloth, and she'd re-stained our old wooden stacking chairs. A bowl of roses on the Dutch dresser effectively outscented the paraffin fumes of our antique camp-cooker.

Andrew was scraping the bottom of his boiled egg. 'Mum, can I have more bread?'

Mike looked up from the book he'd been reading. 'You've had enough. You promised to catch flies.'

'After breakfast,' said Andy, with dignity.

'Greedy guts . . . Okay, I'll get the flies. Sandy's starving.'

'Who's Sandy?' I asked.

'They've found a lizard.' Julia put my coffee on the table. 'Mike's given it first aid, but it isn't looking too happy.'

The lizard was inside a glass mixing bowl on the dresser. The children had made a bed of sand and sunk in a small saucer of water. The little reptile was paying no attention to these amenities. It was lying still, eyes closed, barely breathing. There was a thin strip of sticking plaster wound about its right rear leg.

'Fractured,' Mike told me.

'How do you know?'

'I examined him.'

'Mike, I've told you before . . . you shouldn't experiment . . . '

'Didn't,' Andy came to his elder brother's defence. 'Sandy was sort of limping. And we could feel his leg was broke.'

'That's different,' I had to agree. Besides, Mike's *splint* looked professional as far as I could tell. I'd never been called upon to set a lizard's leg.

'It says,' Mike ran a finger along a line in his book, 'it's a sand lizard, and it's rare 'cause there aren't many dunes left in England.'

'There are no dunes in Craftly.'

'That's why it went to live in the pit. Look dad.'

The picture he showed me did match Sandy's tawny markings.

'He got hurt,' said Andy, 'because somebody chucked a lot of stuff on him.'

'Are you making up stories again?' Julia was trying to keep her face straight.

'Isn't.' Mike closed his book and reached for the marmalade. 'There's lots of rubbish in the pit.'

'What kind?'

'Tins and things.'

I remembered the rumbles and crashes in the night. 'I'd better take a look.'

'Not now.' Julia helped herself to shredded wheat, 'Michael, I need you here. Clive and Mr Cobbler are coming at . . . '

'I know. Plenty of time.'

'There isn't. You lose all sense of time when you're on holiday.'

Julia wasn't wrong, but I didn't like her remark. It meant she was in a flap even before the builders had started. True, the men who'd delivered sand, cement and thermalite blocks had dumped them at the front and back doors so that we'd had to heave passages into the cottage; but then it was what you'd expect of unskilled muscle-men. The builders themselves were bound to be different. To carry out the work detailed in Clive's specifications they'd have to be real craftsmen – qualified bricklayers and plasterers, carpenters and painters – and craftsmen were intelligent people. As to the plumbers and electricians, they'd be sub-contractors – local firms presumably.

'Can I go now?' Andy had already left the table and was making for the door.

'Where to?' asked Julia.

Mike tucked the book under his arm. 'We're taking dad

to the sand pit. Maybe we'll find a snake.'

'If you do, don't bring it home,' Julia capitulated. 'And Michael . . .'

'Don't worry, mum,' said Mike. 'We'll send dad back for your meeting.'

Julia looked at the bowl with the lizard. 'What about Sandy?'

'We're busy, mum. Will you get flies for him? But don't kill them . . . they've got to be a bit alive.'

'Mike, I've other things to do. You must look after your own pets.'

'Please, mum. Sandy isn't really a pet, he's a patient. Look, if you can't catch any midges you can give him green-fly. Your roses are full of them.'

The gardens of the vicarage and Curate's Cottage were enclosed by a low flint wall. The boys and I climbed over on to the public footpath. Briars and brambles had reduced it to a narrow track which ended, a few hundred yards ahead, in a seemingly impenetrable thicket. But Mike had breached it earlier in the morning and proudly led me to the hole he'd cleared. We emerged on level ground with fine old conifers and yew trees.

'It must have been a tree-ery,' said Mike.

'A what?' I asked.

'A tree-ery . . . a place where they grew special trees in the old days.'

'You mean an arboretum.'

'That's Latin,' he told me. 'Our English teacher says we're to use Anglo-Saxon.'

'But there's no such word as tree-ery.'

'There is now,' Andy assured me. 'Mike's just said it.'

Streaky, who'd followed us, suddenly bounded ahead. We went after him, through a copse of sun-dappled trees, but he chose to ignore our whistles and calls. I'd almost lost sight of the dog when he came to a halt, tail up, barking excitedly.

He was waiting for us on the rim of the big hole which no longer looked anything like the sand-pit I had known when I'd done a vet locum in the area. As the boys had said, tons of rubbish – cans, broken bottles, soggy cartons and bursting plastic bags – had been thrown into the pit, transforming it from a countryside feature into an unsightly dump. Most sinister of all were the dented metal drums. They reminded me of newspaper reports that conservationists were protesting against chemical waste being disposed of too casually and carelessly for the good of the population. As the new owner of the nearest country cottage I didn't like it. I didn't like it at all.

'Streaky, stop it!' Mike ordered the dog. 'No!'

Streaky was yelping at something small on the edge of the pit, but keeping his distance. Our dog was much too cautious for engaging in a battle with an unknown form of life. Joining Streaky and my equally alert children I half expected to find a rolled-up hedgehog; but the object of their interest was a large, distinctively marked toad.

'A natterjack!' Mike's big grey eyes were shining with excitement. 'Dad, it's a natterjack.'

'I see.' I grabbed Streaky by the collar.

'But dad! Don't you know 'bout natterjacks? They're special. Same as Sandy, natterjack toads breed in freshwater dune-slacks and . . . '

'There's a dew-pond over there.' If Mike had correctly identified the toad it had probably migrated to a habitat as close as possible to the ideal. Like humans, animals were often forced to adapt to second best environments. The toad sat placidly in the sparse grass, apparently unalarmed by us intruders.

'Dad, you know 'bout the Conservation of Wild Creatures Act of 1975?'

'Not offhand.' A copy of it was probably buried in the

mountain of circulars and veterinary journals which kept flooding into my London surgery. Diplomacy was indicated. It was a bit worrying to stand ignorant before my eleven-year-old. 'What – er – part of the 1975 Act are you thinking of?'

'I think it's page two, where it lists seven animals which are protected by law 'cause they're in danger of dying out. Sandy, my sand lizard, is one of them. And the natterjack's another.'

'Well done, Mike.'

He lay down, facing the toad. Stretching out his arm very slowly, he picked it up and showed it to Andy. 'Isn't he super!' The toad still looked unperturbed. Mike's uncannily delicate touch had always inspired confidence in wild creatures. 'We'll call him Jack . . . or Jackie, in case he's a she.'

'You're not taking it home,' I said firmly.

'Don't know . . . Jackie isn't safe here.' He nodded at the wide dirt-track which ran from somewhere at the back of Craftly High Street to the spot where Streaky had found the toad. 'Where could we put him?'

Mike was right again. If heavy vehicles regularly dumped waste at this point the natterjack was in danger of getting crushed. 'He might be better off on the far side of the pit.'

'What 'bout if he doesn't stay there? Can't we . . . '

'No. A glass jar's the last place for him . . . The pit shouldn't be used as a dump.'

'Can we make a demo?' asked Andy. He'd been keen on demonstrations ever since he'd seen one on television. Perhaps he had a point. These days marching and yelling seemed to produce quicker results than orderly protests through *regular channels.*

'Don't be silly, Andrew.' Mike was stroking the toad's head with one finger. 'Dad'll stop them dumping stuff.'

'How?'

'Well, he can tell the Council 'bout Sandy and Jackie.'

In the past weeks, when we'd been discussing alterations to the cottage and getting the plans approved by the Council, the boys must have gained an exaggerated impression of the Council's powers. I promised the boys I'd see what could be done. But that was too vague for Mike.

'We'll take Jackie to a safe place,' he decided, 'then we'll go to the Manor House and phone.'

'The Council?' asked Andy.

'No, stupid, the Friends of the Earth. They're the ones who look after natterjacks.'

'What'll you say?'

'Well, that we've found important animals and . . . and that we know about them 'cause of the 1975 Act and 'cause dad's a vet . . . and . . . '

'Mike, I'm surprised at you,' I stopped him. 'If this were one of your science projects at school you wouldn't be doing very well, would you?'

'Why not?'

'Because if you want help from conservationists for an animal you must first be sure of your facts. Check whether this toad is what you think it is. Find out whether there's more than one natterjack in the area. Look for . . . '

'S'right, dad. Okay, leave it with us.' Coming from a skinny kid the phrase sounded funny. I reckoned he'd picked it up from our architect. 'You'd better go, dad. We promised mum we'd send you home.'

On my way back to Curate's Cottage the morning seemed to have lost some of its sparkle. A dirty dump, a quarter of a mile from our back door, wasn't my idea of country life. Was that why Clive Astley-Appledore, in his estate agent's capacity, had been so accommodating over the price of the cottage?

Suddenly I was struck by a thought which had been niggling at the back of my mind ever since Julia had engaged Clive as an architect. Surely an architect – a member of the Royal Institute of British Architects – could be struck off the register, just as a veterinary surgeon could be removed from *his* Association's register if he violated the ethics of his profession. Was it ethical for a working architect to be in the estate-agency business? I had my doubts.

Two

Clive, dressed in beige cord slacks and a matching poloneck cashmere sweater, jumped lightly out of his Range Rover. He looked like a professional athlete, face evenly tanned, fair hair expensively styled. 'Ah, Michael,' he greeted me as if he hadn't expected to meet me at the door of my own cottage.

'Sorry about this mess,' I apologized insincerely, 'but your builders dropped the sand bang in front of the door.'

Clive laughed. 'You get used to their ways in my business.'

'Do you mean the estate-agent or the architect business?'

He smiled. 'The estate agency's nothing to do with me.'

'You sold us Curate's Cottage.'

'It wasn't me actually.'

'No?'

'No. You actually bought the place through P & P.'

'Astley-Appledore.'

'P & P Astley-Appledore. Pandora . . . that's my wife, and Pearl, my sister.'

'It was you who negotiated the sale.'

'Think nothing of it, Michael. I reckon I owed you a good turn. Never forgot the way you pinned my dog's leg and saved his life. I wanted you to have Curate's Cottage below market price, and you got it.'

The cottage did look attractive, with the arched windows wreathed in roses and the sun high-lighting the fine craftsmanship of the black and white flint walls. Perhaps my reservations about Clive were churlish. I said, 'There's just one thing that rather bothers me: Simpkins's sand pit.'

'Oh yes?' Clive was all urbane attention.

'It's being used as a rubbish dump.'

'You must be mistaken.'

'I've just been there. Suppose you tell me what's really happening in our immediate neighbourhood.'

Clive looked concerned. 'Surely your solicitor who did the conveyancing gave you all the details. The County Council wanted to buy the pit as a refuse dump a few years back. But Mr Simpkins thought it might upset the village and wouldn't sell. In fact, the local refuse is taken to a place thirty miles away.'

'Well, somebody's dumping into the pit.'

Clive scratched the back of his head. 'Can't understand it. Sure the pit isn't just being filled in? You know that Simpkins has bought the vicarage for his daughter Rosie and her husband? She married a Chinese.'

'So he was saying at the Craftly Arms. Everyone thought he was joking.'

'Not a bit. Simpkins says the Chinese are hard-working people; he'd rather have one of them for a son-in-law than an English layabout on social security . . . Rosie and her husband are planning to turn the vicarage into a sort of country club. You know . . . good food, tennis courts, swimming pool, a nine-hole golf course.'

'That's news to me.'

'Good news, Michael. It'll increase the value of your property.'

'If it comes to pass.'

'I shouldn't be surprised. Mr Choy – Rosie's husband –

should know what he's doing. His father's said to own a chain of restaurants up north.'

'Fine, but meanwhile we've got a refuse dump at the back.'

'Well, I'll see what I can find out about it,' promised Clive.

'So will I.' I didn't mean to be aggressive but that's the effect Clive had on me.

As Clive and I squeezed past the heaps of thermalite blocks and sand into the cottage Builder Arnold Cobbler and another man arrived in a battered Ford Cortina. First out of the car was a very large greyhound.

Julia had turned the kitchen into a conference room. She'd replaced the red breakfast cloth with a soberly brown blanket and put note-pads and ballpens in front of the seats.

'Sit down, gentlemen,' she invited. She had great faith in addressing men as gentlemen, in the touching belief that it would make them behave like gentlemen.

They looked amiable enough. I knew – or so I thought – all about Clive, and he certainly conformed to one's image of a successful young architect. Mr Cobbler, boss of the building firm, was a short, stocky man in his late forties with frank blue eyes and dimpled white hands.

The third member of the party, whom Mr Cobbler introduced as his foreman and bricklayer, was Ernie Butters. Ernie was still under thirty, I guessed, but in his relatively short life he'd succeeded in building up a colossal weight. The loose, hairy sweater he wore obscured whether the huge poundage consisted of muscle or flab, though the general shape suggested a beer-belly with an impressive overhang. In contrast Ernie's swarthy, Italianate head looked small – almost fragile. It was topped by a little knitted hat with a pom-pom in delicate shades of pink and pale blue. He might have borrowed it from a baby.

'Well now,' began Clive. 'Mr Cobbler says that Ernie can start the work first thing tomorrow.'

'Lovely,' Julia smiled. 'What time? I want to get breakfast out of the way.'

Mr Cobbler looked at Ernie. 'Seven-thirty?'

'Okay,' agreed Ernie.

I asked Clive whether he'd discussed with Mr Cobbler the order in which the work was to be carried out. Living in a house while builders were pulling it apart was bound to be inconvenient, but Julia and I had planned the different stages in such a way that family and workmen wouldn't be falling over one another. Hence the bunk-beds, which were easy to shift, and the paraffin cooker which could be used upstairs or even in the old garden shed.

'Mr Cobbler's got the schedule,' Clive assured us.

'You're quite happy about it?' I asked the builder.

'You happy about it?' Mr Cobbler asked Ernie.

'Yeah . . . We start at the top and work down to the bottom.'

'Well, not quite.' Julia picked up our copy of the architect's specifications. 'If you look at page three you'll see that plumbing, central heating and electrical work are to be done first.'

'That's right, Ernie,' said Mr Cobbler. 'The plumber and the electrician will be all over the house. It'll inconvenience madam; so we want to get all that over as soon as possible. Right?'

'Yeah.'

'It shouldn't take more than a week, madam. After that it'll be plain sailing. We'll complete downstairs first, so madam can have her kitchen ship-shape.'

Julia had always wanted a big *living-kitchen* where we could eat and where the boys could entertain their friends – an attractive place with a large pine table and comfortable chairs, with built-in pine cupboards and cooker.

Clive had called it a farmhouse kitchen. To achieve this, the wall between the existing kitchen and scullery would have to be removed. As it was not a weight-bearing wall it would present no problem.

'Ernie, have you got all that?' asked Cobbler.

'Yeah.'

'You can work in with the plumber and the electrician, can't you? Fill in the holes they make.'

Ernie nodded. 'Make good.'

'Right.'

The greyhound, which had arrived in the builders' car, had climbed a mountain of sand outside the open window and was squatting. I watched him produce a turd. The dog contemplated it, like a hypochondriac, turned his back on us and established territorial rights by scratching sand over the turd. His powerful hindlegs made the sand fly far into the kitchen, scattering it on the washed breakfast dishes, on us and the papers on the table.

Ernie got up and closed the window. 'Funny, he don't usually do that.'

Julia's feelings weren't hard to guess. '*We* have a dog too.'

'That's nice.' If Ernie had understood that Julia was warning him off bringing his dog to our cottage he wasn't having any. 'Tango – that's his name, Tango of Toledo – he likes doggies. Play with 'em for hours, he will. Tango's on holiday, see. Couple of weeks; then he goes back to kennels for training.'

'You race him?' I asked.

'Oh yeah. He's a good one.'

'Mr Cobbler,' Julia brushed the sand off her hair, 'it says in the specifications that your men will clean up the place after work . . . day by day.'

'Certainly, madam.'

'You supply the cleaning materials?'

'Oh yes, madam.'

'Good. There's one other thing. We want to keep all the old fittings here . . . the brass door-handles, the iron fire-dogs and basket in the inglenook, the door knockers and the lavatories.'

'Yeah,' said Ernie, 'them seats are nice. Real antiques, same as in Westminster. Can't get wood like that no more.'

'That's why we want to keep them.'

Mr Cobbler nodded. 'Seats like that are warmer than plastic. Ernie said that yours are the same as in the House of Lords. That's where he worked before.'

'Yeah . . . But London's not right for a greyhound, so we moved a couple of years ago. Mind, there's not much life down here – nothing like the West End – but Tango likes it better . . . Wouldn't keep them door-knockers though.'

'Why not Ernie?' asked Mr Cobbler.

'Brass.' The fat boy made it sound like poison.

'What's wrong with brass?'

'Cleaning. Polish, polish all the time. My wife wouldn't give them things houseroom.'

'I will,' Julia told him.

'Ernie's got a point,' said Mr Cobbler. 'There's no need for the modern housewife to spoil her hands with metal polish, not these days. There are things on the market . . . '

'Gloves.'

'To be sure, madam. But why waste your time? We could install a nice litho-chime for you.'

'We don't really want a chime.'

'I was coming to that, madam. The litho's no ordinary chime. It's a special unit, miniaturized by photo-lithography. Scientific, if you get my meaning. When you press the door-bell it plays music. One can order one's own personal tune . . . anything from *Rule Britannia* to *yeh-yeh-yeh*. For you, madam, I'd suggest something nice and tasteful – like *John Brown's Body* or *Home Sweet Home*.'

Clive had closed the meeting with assurances that Mr Cobbler's firm would finish the work within the month. Everything was perfectly straightforward. Julia had stressed that she was certain that all would go well provided Cobbler & Sons Ltd stuck to the time-table and did the various jobs in the order we had agreed.

While she set about sweeping up the sand Tango had flung into the kitchen I accompanied the men out. Now the sun was lighting up the shed; in fact it was an outhouse large enough for garaging three cars, built in the same attractive flint as the cottage. Much of the stonework was hidden behind an ancient wisteria, which would be a picture in spring, and an equally mature fig tree.

'Heard anything about my oak yet?' Clive was asking Mr Cobbler.

'I talked to them on the phone yesterday, Mr Clive. It's at the wharf. German wood's usually pretty reliable, but I think I'll go down to Shoreham and check. We don't want none of that kiln-dried rubbish.'

'Certainly don't,' agreed Clive. 'If it's all right we could go ahead with the job after . . . '

As it was obviously a discussion on another contract I joined Ernie and his greyhound at the Ford.

'Where do you race Tango?' I asked.

'Brighton, though he's done okay on other tracks too . . . Mr Morton, you're a vet, aren't you?'

'Yes.'

'There's a funny thing. Me mates – them's as is part owners of Tango – can't understand it no more than me. Tango's a good dog. Been winning a lot of races for us. But you put 'im in a trap alongside a bitch and he loses every time. Holding back he is; you can see it, plain as daylight.'

I said nothing. Ernie had used one of the standard methods of seeking a free consultation. I'd fallen for it all too often.

'It don't make sense, see. It ain't natural, now is it?'

'What's natural?' I said vaguely. 'I once knew a greyhound who was so scared of rabbits and hares that he threw a fit every time he met one. Even a glove lined with rabbit fur upset him.'

'What 'appened?'

'His owner took him to a dog-psychiatrist in America.'

'He got cured?'

'I reckon the owner got cured. He gave up trying to race the dog.'

Ernie patted his greyhound's rump. 'Well . . . I mean . . . I don't like to say it, but it ain't natural, a dog what can't abide bitches. It ain't nice, is it? Can't you give 'im a pill or something, like they showed on TV? Sex-hormones or something?'

'Why not ask your vet, Ernie?'

'Well, Tango's vet's a lady, see. It's embarrassing like.' He eyed me and then decided that he'd backed a non-starter. 'Reckon I could send the wife along to the vet.'

'Good idea.'

'Mr Morton, about them brass door-knockers.'

'Yes.'

'If you don't want them I'll buy them off you.'

'We do want them.'

'Mate o' mine would pay a good price for them. Maybe you'd like to think about it. And that kitchen dresser. You don't want it, do you? Cost you a bit to have it taken away.'

'My wife likes it.'

'Yeah, but with all them nice new pine units you're putting in it won't look right. You don't want that beat-up old dresser, do you?'

'We think it'll fit in perfectly after I've stripped off the paint.'

'Nasty job, stripping. Lot of work for you, Mr Morton. Tell you what. I'll give you fifty quid for it.'

'No. I don't think we'll sell.'

'Might get you a better price, come to think of it. Mate 'o mine buys pine dressers, nothing else . . . for export, see.'

'Mr Cobbler's coming.' I assumed that Ernie's boss wasn't in on his foreman's business ventures. 'See you tomorrow.'

'Yeah . . . The guv'nor's in on the syndicate.'

'The syndicate?'

'Tango . . . Mr Cobbler's in with me and me mates.'

Well, there was nothing wrong with several men owning a greyhound and sharing the expenses of keeping and racing him. Why let a bias creep into my mind just because the one racing syndicate I'd known before had been a bunch of phoney, disreputable politicians?

As for Tango himself, I guessed Streaky would convince Ernie that another dog wasn't welcome on his territory. Though Streaky always welcomed bitches and sometimes tolerated dogs smaller than himself he'd certainly put up a fierce protest against an animal the size of Tango. That Streaky had never attacked a creature in his life was a secret between dog and family.

Julia was about to make a salad for lunch when Mike and Andy returned accompanied by Six – Sheik Ahmed Habib's sixth son – and a long-legged blonde. They crowded into the kitchen as purposefully as a trade union delegation. Mike told us that Six had invited him and Andy to stay at the Manor House.

'We think it's a good idea,' he told us.

Our boys always were ready to stay at the Manor, which Six's father had turned into the most luxurious country house in the south of England. There was the attraction of an indoor swimming pool, which could be converted into an outdoor one at the turn of a switch; there was a small zoo of exotic animals, a fine library of nature books and a gymnasium.

'Mike, who's invited you two?' asked Julia.

'Six . . . and his parents.'

'Are you sure?'

'Oh mum,' said Andy reproachfully. 'We knew you wouldn't believe us 'bout the Sheik inviting us. That's why we've brought Inga.'

'I'm Inga Porsche,' the blonde introduced herself. 'How do you do?'

'She comes from Germany,' Six told us. 'She's my trainer.'

'For your animals?'

'Not so,' said Inga. 'I have the appointment to train the bodies of Sheik Habib's sons. I show them good-style swims and rides . . . how to make performances in the gymnasium and businesses like . . . like . . . How do you say? I show you, yes?' Inga put her hands on the floor, legs rising towards the ceiling.

'Handstand,' I said.

She gave me a nice smile. 'And this?'

As Julia grabbed her pottery salad bowl, Inga took off.

'Somersault,' said Julia, weakly.

'I vill learn,' Inga assured us. 'Now I take all the children avay?'

Julia and I looked at one another. It wouldn't be our intended family holiday without the boys. On the other hand – what with the builders around – Julia's housekeeping would be simpler without the children.

'If you had a telephone,' said Six, 'my father would have phoned you personally, sir.'

After that we had to accept the invitation.

'Ve vill visit you,' promised Inga.

Mike took the bowl with the lizard off the dresser. 'Don't worry mum, we'll look after Sandy . . . See you.'

'Wait. You'd better take a few things . . . '

'Ve must go to eat,' said Inga. 'I come later to fetch your sons' clothes. Yes?'

'We'll be at the sand-pit anyway,' Mike told us. 'You know the toad, dad? Well, it *is* a natterjack. So, like you said, we'll see whether there's more of them.'

'All right. But be careful; there's a lot of broken glass around.'

Six glanced at his bionic-woman trainer. 'She knows about the glass. She'll pick it up. Good bye, sir.'

They'd trooped out, leaving us – not for the first time – somewhat speechless, when Andy came rushing back. He put his arms round Julia's waist and hugged her. 'Mum, we'll be back every morning.'

'That's nice, darling.' Julia was obviously glad that Andy, for once, was behaving like the little boy he was. 'Have a nice time.'

'It'll be super, mum. But Mike said we've got to go home every day 'cause of the builders.'

'What about the builders, Andy?'

'Mike says we've got to watch them.'

'See how they're getting on?'

'No . . . Watch they don't do funny things.'

'What do you mean?'

'Mike 'n me watched them last year.'

Builders had in fact worked at the Manor House while our boys had been staying with the Habibs.

'What happened?' I asked. Unlike Mike, the inveterate teller of embroidered stories, Andy could be relied upon to give us plain facts.

'Every time we switched on a light the burglar alarm went off.'

'We're not having an alarm, Andy. We don't need one.'

'And they put the dishwater in the Sheik's bedroom.'

'We're not having a dishwasher either.'

'Bet builders can do other things . . . says Mike.'

Three

Julia and I were at breakfast when we heard the clip-clop of a horse's hooves. The light in the kitchen dimmed as the chestnut appeared at the open window. The rider, a lean grey-haired woman in black jacket and bowler hat, leaned in.

'Morning. You the Mortons?'

Julia said we were.

'Kath Greatorex . . . stress on the second syllable. Had a report from your son.'

'Yes?' A spasm of guilt shot through my mind. Had one of our kids reported us to the Society for the Prevention of Cruelty to Children? I couldn't remember when we'd last smacked one or other. 'Mike?'

'Right,' said the rider briskly. 'Michael Morton, junior. He's found a natterjack toad in your sand-pit, I understand.'

I said, yes, Mike had found a toad but I wasn't sure that it was a natterjack. And the sand-pit wasn't ours.

'Soon get to the bottom of it,' Miss Greatorex assured us. 'Local team – we're the Friends of the Earth – are going to work on it.'

'Mike will appreciate that,' said Julia. 'Won't you come in for a cup of coffee?'

'No thanks. Young Bumper – my brother's horse – is

a bit frisky . . . Whoa! Steady boy! Would like a word with your son.'

'He's staying with friends, at the Manor House.'

'Arabs . . . Place is full of exotic pets. No home for a natterjack toad.'

'I'm sure Mike's left the toad at the pit.'

'No home for a natterjack either. Place is a disgrace.'

I agreed that it was.

'Lancashire, the sandhills, that's the proper habitat for natterjacks and sand lizards. It's a Site of Special Scientific Interest... which hasn't stopped Sefton Borough Council from letting Fred Pontin build there; a holiday camp.'

'That's a shame.' Julia meant it.

'The fight goes on.' Miss Greatorex tightened the reins on her restive horse. 'Exciting development finding such rare creatures at Craftly . . . Exciting if a colony of them settled here. First things first though. Got to get the pit cleaned up.'

I agreed, but suggested that the Friends of the Earth would be in a stronger position if more sand lizards and natterjacks were found on the site. Miss Greatorex promised that her team would join our boys in the search.

'Hope your sons will join our Association.' She took some papers from her jacket pocket and let them flutter into the kitchen. 'Hope you're not going to do too much to this cottage. Upsets the owls and the field-mice, you know.'

'Any other wildlife here?' I asked.

'Bats. And wood-pigeons of course. Shouldn't bother growing vegetables or fruit in your garden. Wood-pigeons eat the lot. Trouble about being a Friend of the Earth... got to watch the damned pigeons get so fat they can hardly take off, and can't do a bloody thing. Not allowed to shoot them.'

At seven-thirty sharp the builders arrived in force: Ernie, a very small elderly man he introduced as his mate Ferret, and Greyhound Tango in the Ford. Dickie, the plumber, drove up in a van. He was a tall, stringy man in his thirties with a sour face and remarkably large hands. Another van brought Sparks, a young electrician, who looked young and efficient.

The first thing that happened was that our dog squared up to the Ford and made it clear that the greyhound was going to stay in it.

'Don't matter to us,' Ernie assured me. 'Me mate'll take Tango walks.'

I carried Julia's sewing machine into the outhouse. She'd planned to leave the cottage to the men and make curtains, either in the shed or in the garden, depending on the weather. It was going to be another warm, sunny day. I took my time looking at the chores I'd have to tackle out of doors. The grass had grown knee-high, but with regular cutting it would probably turn into a good lawn. The gravelled drive between us and the vicarage needed weeding and I'd have to take the briars off the old standard roses. Then there were the sycamore trees, aggressive messy giants which would take over the whole garden if I let them. I wouldn't wait until the autumn before cutting them back. In my experience one could take liberties with sycamores; it was almost impossible to kill them.

By nine o'clock the banging from the cottage indicated that our builders were hard at work. A load of copper piping had been delivered and Ferret was rushing in and out with bits of old and new plumbing. I decided to go to the village, buy the most necessary garden tools and order a daily paper.

As I unlocked the car Ernie's head appeared at the bathroom window.

'Bentley?' he asked.

'No, it's an old Armstrong-Siddeley.'

'Nice.' His beer-belly came to rest on the ledge. 'Cost you a bit, didn't it?'

'It didn't. I inherited it.'

'Some people have all the luck.'

'From an old lady who never paid what she owed me.'

Ernie's head, topped by the pink and blue knitted hat, tilted thoughtfully. 'Big car. Cost a lot to run.'

'Cheaper than buying a new car.'

'Yeah . . . Heavy on petrol though. Wouldn't do more 'n eighteen miles to the gallon. Want to sell it?'

'No.'

'Got a mate who might be interested.'

'Ernie, I'm not selling my Armstrong. I like it.'

'Yeah . . . well, you want to think about it guv'nor. Could have a word with me mate. Give you a good price, he would.'

As a part-owner of Craftly the village interested me more than ever. I saw things I hadn't noticed before, such as the ancient stone roof on the church, the variety of High Street architecture which ranged from crooked Tudor to Georgian, and the boxes of flowers above the shops.

I parked the Armstrong in a side-street and walked into Miss Godley's shop – a true village emporium stocked with anything from knitting wool and underwear to sweets and newspapers. Miss Godley was a neat little country-woman who could have been any age between forty and sixty. As Craftly's only newsagent she worked all hours, even keeping the shop open on Sundays and holidays. She was talking to her twin sister, Mrs Glib, who was running the post office together with her husband.

'Nice to see you, Mr Morton.' Miss Godley had been welcoming ever since I'd removed a cyst from her cat's neck.

'Lovely day,' said Mrs Glib. 'Makes a difference when you're settling in.'

'It'll take a while. At the moment we're cam[torn] Curate's Cottage.'

'Ah yes,' Mrs Glib nodded. 'We heard you had the builders in.'

'That's right.'

The twins exchanged looks, Miss Godley absent-mindedly stroking the big grey cat which was lying on the counter among the women's magazines. Old as Tom was, his coat shone like polished pewter, due – I guessed – to regular absentminded caresses. 'Cobblers?' Miss Godley's question hung in the air.

'Yes.'

'Then it's Clive Astley-Appledore looking after the work for you . . . What a nuisance.'

'Why?'

'The Summer Fair, Mr Morton,' said Mrs Glib. 'Clive's wife promised to do the floats. But if Pandora's got to run the office she'll be too busy.'

'Our building work shouldn't take Clive that much time.'

'It isn't just your cottage,' explained Miss Godley. 'There's all the building they're doing at their own place.'

'What's that?'

'He didn't mention it to you? Well, I suppose Clive's keeping quiet. He knows the village isn't keen on his plans. He had trouble getting them passed . . . Our Parish Council's against turning old buildings into modern offices.'

'Is that what he's doing?'

'It's the coach house at Appledore Place. That's where he's going to move the estate agency and his studio. Mind you, Mr Morton, he's not allowed to put up them nasty concrete units. The Council's making him use the existing flint walls and natural materials.'

'Timber?' I remembered the oak Clive and Cobbler had discussed.

said Miss Godley. 'Well, we don't want … look like Nether Craftly, do we? That awful …arket. It's bad enough that the Church's sold the …icarage. Never know what'll become of it.'

'Didn't Mr Simpkins buy it? I heard his son-in-law's turning it into a country club.'

'Well, Mr Morton,' Glib and Godley exchanged glances. 'If you're asking our opinion . . . we'll be lucky if we live to see it. Once the Chinese move into a place . . . We've seen what happened in Nether Craftly.'

What I had seen at Nether Craftly hadn't shocked me. The supermarket, pleasantly built on the edge of the recreation ground, had replaced a messy second-hand furniture depot. And since a Chinese family had taken over the fish and chips business the shop was cleaner and smelled better.

'It's not that we in Craftly mind foreigners,' said Miss Godley, 'I mean we had the Romans and the Normans, didn't we? It's just foreign ways.'

'And it isn't kind to *them*,' Mrs Glib supported her sister, 'making them settle down here. They never really do, if you know what I mean, Mr Morton. You take our vicar's wife. Been here these twenty years, has Carmen, but she still feels the cold something terrible . . . and she still hasn't joined the Women's Institute or the Mothers' Union. Mind you, Mr Morton, Carmen Gilbey's a nice lady; but she'd be better off in her own country . . . I mean, Craftly isn't Majorca, is it?'

Miss Godley accepted my newspaper order, in principle. No trouble delivering to Curate's Cottage, but what could *she* do if certain papers weren't printed at all or failed to arrive from London? She hated disappointing her customers. 'Industrial action! If our dad – who started this business – knew about all them strikes he'd turn in his grave. I mean papers like *The Times*! First it was late for breakfast.' It seemed as if Miss Godley was accusing *The Times* of bad manners. 'Now it don't turn up at all.'

'We've always taken the *Daily Telegraph*,' Mrs Glib told me. 'A good, sensible paper with proper opinions. Now there's days when there's blank spaces instead of pictures.'

'That's why I've advised my customers to change their orders,' said Miss Godley. 'If you must have a London paper, Mr Morton, you'd be safer with the *Mirror*.'

'Not quite the same as *The Times*.'

'True. Mind you, I think a daily paper's a waste of time . . . especially when you're busy with builders about the place. Still . . . you know best. But if I were you I'd avoid a paper that's got to come down from London.'

'The railway men,' said Mrs Glib. 'You never know when they'll go on strike again. If it's not the papers it's the trains. And when people don't get their letters they blame my post office.'

'The postmen have been on strike too,' Miss Godley reminded Mrs Glib.

'I didn't say they were perfect.'

'And the telephone engineers.'

'And the hospital workers,' Mrs Glib threw at Miss Godley. 'Not to speak of the waste disposal men and the car workers.'

'All I'm saying is,' said Miss Godley, 'we've put up too long with the rest of the country. What we need down here is devolution . . . run things our way and stand on our own feet. You take my advice, Mr Morton. Forget about London. If you let me send you our local papers you'll be sure of a regular delivery. You'll have the *Craftly Echo* by eight o'clock every morning, the *Craftly Clarion* every Thursday. And if it's journals you want, there's the *Craftly Stable and Stud* for you . . . and for your wife, the *Craftly Woman*.'

When I left Miss Godley's shop it wasn't entirely without a sense of achievement. We'd reached a compromise; she'd supply us with one national daily paper and one local, on the understanding that I'd accept a second local paper whenever the London newspapers failed to arrive.

I walked down the High Street to Simpkin's Hardware. It had once been a shop of pots and pans, but after Simpkins had become a County Councillor he'd spread his commercial wings. The hardware had been relegated to a shed at the back, while the much expanded front had become a showroom for garden and farm equipment.

Mr Simpkins, a little man with pink cheeks and thick white hair, proudly showed me his selections of spades and rakes, saws and hedge-cutters. There wasn't much he wouldn't be able to supply on the spot.

I picked the most necessary tools plus a bunch of leaflets giving details of expensive machines such as lawn mowers. Unlike shopping in London it was all very leisurely and enjoyable. I might have forgotten to ask about the sand-pit if Mr Choy, our neighbour at the vicarage, hadn't walked in.

Simpkins introduced his son-in-law with a mixture of defiance and pride. He talked of Choy's plans for the country club, Choy – with engaging modesty – said he hoped his business would prosper sufficiently to make these future plans feasible. I asked whether the sand-pit was a part of these plans.

'The pit no longer yields a commercial amount of sand,' said Mr Choy, in impeccable English. 'Therefore it would be pleasant to incorporate it in a nine-hole golf course.'

'Meanwhile it's being used as a dump.'

Mr Choy nodded. 'It is unfortunate. People are so untidy.'

'My impression is that it's being used for organized large-scale waste disposal.'

'Not by our Council, Mr Morton,' Simpkins assured

me. 'I put my foot down, despite the fact that there's no other suitable local site. Our waste is being taken all the way to Bleep . . . thirty miles away.'

'Then who *is* using your pit?'

Simpkins gazed at his son-in-law. 'We'll have to go into it, won't we Lee?'

'It's a busy time for all of us,' stated Mr Choy with – what I took to be – an enigmatic Chinese smile.

After a ploughman's lunch Julia returned to her sewing and I went to dig a patch of weeds which must have once been a vegetable garden. Despite Kath Greatorex's warning of fat, predatory wood-pigeons I intended to grow some winter greens. Streaky, sure I'd invented a new game, stayed with me all afternoon, digging up a weird collection of antique ink-bottles, broken pottery and rusty cans. If ever I'd doubted our wisdom in buying a country place, the peaceful, sunny afternoon convinced me that we'd done the right thing. There was much to be said for feeling not just well but positively strong and healthy. When Julia called me I was surprised to find that some of the workmen were about to go home. Time had passed unbelievably quickly.

'Michael! Come upstairs!' Julia sounded upset. 'Hurry!'

The electrician's and plumber's vans were moving off. At the back door Ernie was stripping off his overalls.

I found Julia in the bathroom gazing at a scene of formidable devastation. The floor was littered with old pipes and rubble, pipes and cables were hanging from the walls, the tank of the loo was standing on its side and the precious wooden seat has gone.

'Michael, nothing works.' Julia was almost in tears.

'Well, you've got to expect a certain amount of . . . '

'The loo isn't flushing . . . '

'We'll use buckets of water.'

'The water's turned off.'

'We can turn it on.'

'Can't. The pipes aren't connected. Why couldn't they put in the new pipes before ripping out the old? And just look at this mess! They're supposed to clean up after work.'

'What do you want me to do?'

'Oh Michael! Ernie's got to do something about it. Catch him. Don't let him get away. Please!'

I rushed downstairs and just managed to stop the Ford. 'Ernie, you haven't finished for the day, have you?'

He popped his head out of the car window. 'Seven-thirty to four-thirty . . . them's the working hours.'

'What about the loo?'

'Plumber's job . . . He's gone.'

'We must have water.'

'There's the tap in the scullery,' said Ferret. He was sitting in the back with the greyhound.

'Is it working?'

'Dunno,' shrugged Ernie.

'Better see that it does,' I told him.

'Plumber's job,' he grumbled. But he did squeeze out of the car.

I followed him and Ferret into the kitchen and scullery. Here also the walls were full of holes, the floor covered in dust and masonry.

Ernie ran his fingers along a pipe under the sink. 'There's a piece missing.'

'Isn't that it? On the floor.'

'Yeah. Anybody can fix it.'

'I could fix it if I had the tools,' I told him. 'How about lending me yours?'

'Can't do that. It's against the rules . . . Look 'ere, we'll do the job for you. But it's overtime, so it'll cost you extra.'

'All right.' I wasn't going to argue with Ernie. I'd take

the matter up with the boss. 'And do a bit of clearing up too, will you?'

'That's Ferret's job.'

'Why hasn't he done it?'

'Save us!' Ernie sighed. 'He had to walk Tango didn't he? Seeing as the dog wasn't allowed out of the car.'

'He can do it now, can't he?'

'On overtime. That'll cost you extra.'

'Look here,' I spoke quietly, determined to keep my temper. 'I know it's a bit difficult for you, but we're living here and you've got to organize the work accordingly. We can manage without electricity for a week . . . '

'Electrician's job.'

'I know . . . But we can't do without water . . . '

'Fixing it, ain't I?'

'What I'm saying goes for the job from beginning to end. My wife has to keep house as best she can, and it would help her if you cleared up . . . as Mr Cobbler promised.'

'Yeah. Ferret, get me tools, will ya?'

Ernie didn't have the right spanners, but he was quite clever in improvising. While Ferret cleared the centre of the floor with a piece of wood, he managed to get the pipes joined up, the tap functioning. It took less than half an hour.

As Ernie was packing up again I asked him what had happened to the toilet seat in the bathroom.

'Isn't it up there?' he asked.

'No. My wife can't find it.'

'Plumber must 'ave put it somewhere.'

I followed the two men to the car. Ernie, despite his bulk, moved as nimbly as if he were walking on eggs. As Ernie opened the boot of the Ford to let Ferret put in the tools I moved aside a ground sheet. Under it lay our mahogany toilet seat.

'Funny.' Ernie lifted it out, unabashed. 'Reckon the

plumber must 'ave dropped it in by mistake.'

'Perhaps you told him you could get me a good price for it.'

He smiled at me. 'Yeah.' He gave me the seat, closed the boot and remained standing in front of me as if one of us had forgotten something.

I said, 'See you in the morning.'

'Yeah.' He watched a singing thrush on the wisteria, apparently in no hurry to go home.

I suddenly realized that the fat monster was expecting me to tip him for having done the job that would cost me extra. What was I to do? If I gave him something he'd expect me to make a habit of it, if I didn't he was in a position to make our life irritating if not worse.

I slapped Ernie on the shoulder. 'You've been most helpful. I really appreciate it.'

'Yeah?' He lumbered off, undoubtedly trying to work out whether or not I was the kind who'd come up to his expectations at the end of the job. 'If you want to sell them old lead pipes in the house, mate o' mine'll give you a good price.'

Julia, determined to keep out of the workmen's way, had brought the breakfast upstairs. She'd set the table in the now unoccupied boys' bedroom, which had a fine view of the church and the hills.

We were enjoying the fragrant scent of the Albertina and the golden sunlight on the trees when an almighty crash below almost made me drop my coffee cup. The floor under us shivered. Inside the walls there was a noise that sounded as if the old mortar were disintegrating. A second crash, even louder, brought Julia to her feet.

'Michael, what are they doing?'

'Carrying on where they left off last night.'

'Don't be funny . . . please. Let's see.'

We got to the kitchen in time for the next crash. A lump

of bricks and mortar came tumbling down. The dust in the air was so thick that we could hardly see Ernie's head through the hole between kitchen and scullery.

'What are you doing?' asked Julia, despairingly.

'We got to knock out them walls, right?'

'Not yet,' I told him. 'The plan is that the upstairs part is to be finished before you start the alterations down here.'

'If you want me and me mate to stop, it's all right by us. You're the one what's paying.'

'You know the work-plans. Where's the plumber . . . and the electrician?'

'Dunno.'

'You are the foreman?'

'Yeah. But you'll have to ask Mr Cobbler. No use calling him before nine-thirty though.'

'What's his home number?'

'Dunno.'

'Surely, you must be able to get hold of the boss,' Julia pressed Ernie.

'Nah. The guv'nor's number's ex-directory.' He put down the sledge-hammer he'd been wielding. 'Come on, Ferret.'

The two of them walked out.

'What do we do now?' Julia was almost in tears.

'No use upsetting yourself because the plumber and the electrician are late. They'll turn up.'

I helped Julia clear the debris from the kitchen. Outside Ernie and Ferret were living the good life. Ernie, still wearing his woolly hat, had taken off his shirt and was displaying great hunks of sunburnt flesh. While Ferret was brushing Greyhound Tango, Ernie was helping himself from big plastic food-boxes and thermos jars. I watched him put away chicken legs, sandwiches, a pie, mugs of liquid and dollops of icecream. When he'd finished the feast he lay back, surrounded by his food containers and went to sleep. At least, I assumed he was sleeping, from the even rise and fall of his naked belly.

At ten o'clock men and greyhound were still lying in the grass and none of the other trades had turned up. Something had to be done. I went to the public call box in the village and dialled Clive's number. Surely it was the architect's job to supervise builders and see that the work was done according to plan.

Clive's wife answered. She was sorry her husband wouldn't be able to help; he'd gone to Scotland for a couple of days. She didn't think he'd mind if I called Mr Cobbler.

I called Mr Cobbler. There was a click at the other end of the line, followed by a genteel woman's voice. 'This is Cobbler & Sons Ltd. Owing to staff holidays this office is closed until the end of August. We apologize for any inconvenience. If you wish to leave a message it will be recorded.' Would speaking to the answer-phone get me anywhere? 'When you hear a click,' continued the voice, 'please give your name and address, followed by the message. Please speak slowly and clearly.'

I didn't feel hopeful, but I did as I was told, demanding the return of plumber and electrician and a visit from Mr Cobbler.

Back at the cottage Ernie was again knocking chunks out of the wall. Julia told me he'd been at it for ten minutes. Another ten minutes later he told Ferret to take the dog for a walk and went out for a rest. Off came his overalls and shirt, out came the thermos with the icecream.

I joined him. 'Any news?'

'What news?' He went on shovelling the icecream into his mouth.

'Heard anything from the electrician or plumber?'

'Naw. No good asking me where they're from. I dunno. They're sub-contractors.'

'If we got the electrics working you wouldn't have to

knock down walls. You could use an electric cutter, couldn't you? It would be better for our house and easier for you.'

'I don't mind.'

'I do. The way you're doing it could damage the walls upstairs.'

'You want to tell the guv'nor.'

'He doesn't seem to be around.'

'Yeah. He's gone to Shoreham.'

I reckoned that he *and* our architect had gone to Shoreham to inspect the timber for Clive's offices and studio. I left the suntanned mountain of flesh resting in the long grass.

By the end of the working day Ernie had enlarged the hole to a square yard and spent four and a half hours eating and sleeping, while Ferret – too busy to clear up the rubble – had groomed and exercised Tango.

At four-thirty sharp the men climbed into their Ford and Ernie, perhaps moved by a kindly impulse, told me he might be seeing the guv'nor.

'Will you ask him to call in the morning.'

'No 'arm telling him. But 'e's got other jobs too.'

As the Ford moved off with a dusty racing start, Miss Kath Greatorex came trotting up our drive. This time she was riding an elderly white horse.

'Mr Morton, I've got a message from your sons. We have, in fact, found a whole colony of natterjack toads. Isn't it exciting! No sand lizards though . . . Now, we've got to do something about the pit. We've been questioning the people in the cottages on the other side. Seems somebody's tipping in rubbish every Wednesday and Friday . . . It's Wednesday today. We're going to find out who they are. You with us?'

'Yes, of course.'

'Good man . . . They come by night, so I want you at

the pit by twelve. Bring your shotgun.' She'd turned the horse and was trotting off.

'I haven't got a shotgun,' I called after her.

'Not to worry! I'll borrow my brother's.'

Four

'It is a night for adorating nature,' declared Inga. Sensibly, the Habib family had not permitted our sons and Six to *adorate* nature at the sand-pit at midnight. By way of a compromise Six's bionic-woman trainer had been sent along as a deputy. The boys, having appointed themselves guardians of the natterjack toad, considered that they had the right to know what was going on at the toads' chosen home. 'I love the peacyness of the stars.'

'Twaddle,' muttered Kath Greatorex. 'Sentimental rubbish.' She was in a bad mood because I'd made her leave the shotgun in her car.

It was a pleasant night though, warm and scented with clover and meadowsweet. It would have been quite light if the clouds hadn't been chasing across the moon. The sounds of nocturnal life were all around us; not far from the pit a dog-fox was calling the vixen, an owl was hooting and a dog was barking at a sleepless cow.

'Had a word with Simpkins,' Kath Greatorex told us. 'Cagey customer, Hardware Simpkins. Known him all my life. Never really trusted him.'

'What did he say?' I asked.

'That he has no interest in the pit. Belongs to that Chinese now. Man can't just stop being interested in his own land.'

We all heard the rumbling and backed into the shadow of some blackthorns. The hum of powerful engines was coming closer and presently two huge square shapes came lumbering towards the pit.

'We'll get them when they get out,' muttered Kath.

The two juggernauts stopped and then backed up against the pit. As we waited for the drivers to emerge, the great boxes behind the cabins lifted skyward and eventually tilted over the tip. The juggernauts, like defecating elephants, disgorged a deluge of waste but their drivers never left the cabins.

'Must find out who they are,' Kath stomped to the transports, in front of me and Inga.

If the drivers heard her shout or saw us they gave no sign. They hauled their boxes back and drove off. We'd seen no owners' names on the juggernauts because, at the crucial moments, the clouds had cut off the light. And by the time I'd put on my torch the transports were too far away for me to make out their number plates.

'Bungled it,' stated Kath. 'Know better next time. See you here Friday night.'

I said, 'There must be an easier way of finding out who they are.'

'Always better to argue from knowledge,' said Kath. 'Better have the facts before we make a fuss.'

'Is right,' agreed Inga. 'Next time I jump on the leader yes?'

I told the two of them that I was against acrobatics as well as shotguns. 'These men are – more likely than not – doing a perfectly legitimate job.'

'Not when they're endangering protected wildlife,' snapped Kath. 'Are you withdrawing your support, Mr Morton?'

'No.'

'Until Friday then.' She got into her ancient Mini Traveller and bumped off along the track to the village.

I offered to see Inga home, but Six's trainer assured me that her judo and karate would cope in the *unbelievable possibility* of an attack.

I was walking home along the track when I saw a square parcel in my path. It was a cardboard box, professionally sealed with plastic tape and it looked brand new. Thinking of the mad bombers and terrorists of this world I decided to leave it where it lay. Should I inform the police? I didn't feel like going to the call-box in the village at half past one in the morning, yet the parcel made me feel uneasy.

While I was trying to make up my mind, the lights of a car were coming towards me very slowly and cautiously. I faded into the bushes. I reckoned that one of the juggernaut drivers had dropped the parcel from his cab and that someone was about to collect it. A drug-racket at the doorstep of our country home?

The car stopped and a person emerged. Leaving the lights on he went along the track, the beam of his torch raking the ground. I didn't think he would see me. The darkness had deepened and a few big raindrops came splashing down.

The torch-beam, criss-crossing the track was coming nearer. I could make out the shape of the man – an outstandingly bulky shape. The beam located the parcel, he bent down and picked it up. Then, with surprising speed, he trotted back to his car.

Suddenly there was a break in the clouds and for a moment the figure of the man became clearly visible. He was wearing a hat with a pom-pom. But even if he hadn't worn it I'd have recognized our own foreman builder, Ernie.

Five

Our builders had arrived, as usual, at seven-thirty. From eight to nine they'd knocked off for their first breakfast, and then Ferret and Tango had set off for a cross-country walk. Ever since, Ernie had stood in the half-demolished kitchen watching the drive and yawning his head off.

'What are your plans this morning?' asked Julia, trying to be tactful.

'Waiting for the guv'nor.'

'He's definitely coming?'

'He said he was.' Ernie yawned.

'Tired?' I asked.

'Yeah.'

'You had a late night.'

He looked at me through half-closed eyes. 'Yeah.'

'Found something useful at the sand-pit?'

Ernie's eyes snapped wide open. 'Dunno.'

'Just a little something that fell off the back of a lorry. Brave of you to pick it up. There might have been a bomb in it.'

'Dunno.' He shuffled his surprisingly small feet like a delinquent schoolboy. 'I went there for a mate o' mine, see.'

At ten-thirty Mr Cobbler, looking well-scrubbed and dynamic, arrived. He looked at his drooping Ernie and slapped him on the shoulder. 'How's it going then?'

'Okay.'

I said, 'Ernie's being optimistic.'

'Oh?' Mr Cobbler looked at the dusty, devastated kitchen. 'Won't hold you up, Ernie. Carry on with the work upstairs.'

Ernie sloped off and we sat down at the table. Julia picked up Clive's specifications and Mr Cobbler produced his copy – a dirty, dog-eared one – from his briefcase.

'What would seem to be the trouble?' asked Cobbler.

'It doesn't *seem*,' said Julia, 'it is.'

'I see, madam.'

'Good, then you'll agree that your men are way behind with the work. By now the plumbing and electrical work should be finished. Instead we're still flushing the lavatory with buckets of water and only one tap's functioning. We still have to use pressure lamps and candles. And instead of completing one part of the house before starting down here your men have ripped the whole place apart.'

'It can't go on like this,' I supported Julia.

'I will admit,' said Cobbler, softly, 'there have been hold-ups.'

'Why?'

'It's our suppliers. They sent the wrong pipes, so the plumber couldn't get on with it. I've been on to them.'

'When are they going to send the right pipes?'

'Well . . . the ones in Mr Clive's specifications won't be available for several months.'

Julia gasped. 'Have you told Clive?'

'He's on a job in Devon right now . . . But I think we can probably get round the problem. The pipes they've sent us won't do for the radiators Mr Clive's specified – the Mayfair Slims, that is – but they'd be all right if you agreed to changing to Buckingham Royal Thins. You see, the Buckingham Royals are always available.'

'Are they more expensive?' I asked.

'Afraid they are, Mr Morton. There isn't much in it though . . . about £10 per radiator.'

'Plus Value Added Tax?'

'Plus VAT,' he agreed, 'and slightly higher plumbing costs. I can't deny it . . . it'll cost you extra, but if you want the job completed while you're here we don't really have much choice.'

'If we agree, the job will be completed on time?'

'Certainly.'

A truck crunched into our drive and we went out, Julia with anticipation in her eyes.

'It's the kitchen units,' she said happily.

We watched the driver and his mate unload the louvred wood units on top of the builders' sand. If I didn't put them into the shed they'd look beat up long before the carpenter put them in where they belonged.

Mr Cobbler had taken the delivery note and was ticking off drawers and cupboard fronts.

'That's the lot,' said the driver. 'Sign for it at the bottom.'

'Hang on.' Cobbler looked inside the truck. 'Where are the hinges?'

'No hinges. Mr Smith said to tell you hinges aren't available . . . not for this model.'

'What's he got then?'

'The brass fleur-de-lis, but them's for the Queensberry units like. Mr Smith said he might be able to lay his hands on the fleur-de-lis but he can't guarantee it.'

'Then we'll have to find different units,' said Julia.

'Don't you worry, madam,' soothed Mr Cobbler. 'We'll get round this little problem.' He gave the delivery-note copy back to the driver. 'Tell Mr Smith I'll be in touch.'

'You don't want the fleur-de-lis hinges then?'

'Yes, if he can get them by the end of next week.'

'Mr Smith said to tell you, they'll cost you extra.' He

started the engine and shot off, scattering sand all over the kitchen units.

'No harm in ordering the hinges.' Mr Cobbler gave Julia a wise smile. 'Meanwhile I'll try one or two other suppliers.'

I said, 'We knew that certain things are hard to get. That's why we asked Clive to order everything weeks ago . . . when the building permission came through.'

'Not to worry sir, I'm used to getting round little problems like that. All sorted out now.' He turned to his car. 'I'll see to the radiators.'

'Mr Cobbler,' Julia stopped him. 'What about the plumber? He should be getting on with the pipe-work.'

'Well . . . he's on another job now.'

'But we must have him *now*.'

'I'll find somebody else.'

'And the electrician?'

'He's a sub-contractor. It's difficult to get hold of him in working hours. You could phone him in the evening.'

'No, Mr Cobbler,' I said, '*you* do it. We haven't got a telephone yet. Besides I don't want to interfere in your job.'

'Righto.'

'We want the electrician here in the morning.'

'One can't be sure with sub-contractors . . . However, I'll work out something for you.'

'That still leaves the order of work. Could you remind your men that they're supposed to complete upstairs before they wreck any more on the ground floor?'

'That's all right, sir. Ernie knows about that.'

Ernie and Ferret, who had busily chiselled holes into the upstairs walls while thc boss had been around, spent the rest of the day in stop-go rhythm – half an hour's work to one hour's eating and sun-bathing. Even pale little Ferret, who was regularly letting the greyhound out of the car, was getting a pink face and fore-arms.

The day after Cobbler's visit man and mate began with an early breakfast, which lasted from seven-thirty to nine. Then, in the absence of plumber and electrician, Ernie produced a blow-torch and went at the pipes while Ferret went to work on the wiring.

Julia and I, fearful of upsetting the activities, crept into the shed and consulted.

'Michael, do you think they know what they're doing?'

'They've got Clive's drawings there.'

'I know. But can they read the drawings?'

'Let's hope they do.'

'It's not good enough, Michael. It says in the specifications that all work's to be carried out by qualified craftsmen. Ernie can't be a qualified bricklayer and a qualified plumber, can he?'

'It's not impossible.'

'Then why didn't *he* start the plumbing?'

'Secret of the building trade, no doubt.'

'And Ferret. He's supposed to be a labourer, not an electrician. Michael, what *are* we going to do?'

'You mean, what am *I* going to do. Well, for a start I'm going to keep an eye on the men . . . see how they're doing the job.'

'Thank you darling.'

Cheered by Julia's faith in me I went upstairs and checked Ernie's pipework against Clive's drawing. It looked correct except inside the wall which accommodated a water pipe as well as the wiring for a light above the wash-basin.

'This wire seems rather close to the pipe,' I said to Ernie. Ferret continued knocking in staples to hold the wire to the wall.

'Dunno.' Ernie downed tools and put his hands on his hips. 'We do it like on the drawing.'

'I know. But it doesn't seem a good idea.'

'Why's that then?'

'Because if the pipe sprung a leak and water got into the wiring somebody could be electrocuted.'

'Yeah?'

'It's got to be changed.'

'That'll cost you extra.'

'No, it won't. You've got plenty of slack on the wire. It can come down on the other side of the mirror.'

'Okay . . . Ferret, you 'eard. Architects,' snorted Ernie. 'If they ever did the work theirselves they wouldn't do them stupid things.'

'Wire isn't long enough,' said Ferret.

'Sure it is.' Ernie grabbed it. 'Give it a pull.'

'Wait!' I stopped him. 'Is the current off?'

'Dunno.' Ernie yanked the wire out.

There was a mighty flash and a bang and the two men collapsed in a heap on the floor.

God knows what would have happened if they hadn't worn rubber-soled shoes. As it was they'd got away with no more than a scare.

'Save us!' muttered Ernie.

'You won't be so lucky next time,' I told him. 'But there needn't be a next time if you remember to switch off the juice at the main.'

'Yeah.' Under his tan, Ernie was looking rather washed out. 'Come on, Ferret, what we need's a cuppa.'

The tea-break extended into the lunch break. Between two and three the men sat under a tree with Clive's working drawings spread across their knees. Then Tango began to bark somewhat hysterically and they went to pacify him.

When the greyhound wouldn't stop Ernie opened the car door and let him out. I was expecting Ferret to put the lead on him when Tango gave a high-pitched yelp and went racing down the drive. He must have spotted a rabbit and he was now in hot pursuit.

Ferret took off after Tango. Ernie got into the car and went after them. I didn't expect to see the men again – certainly not until the morning – when the car returned, well after working hours. Ernie got out and watched me cut the branch of a sycamore.

'Want us to get on with it?' he asked, at last.

'That would cost us extra, wouldn't it?'

'No.'

'It's after your working hours.'

'Yeah . . . but we was after Tango, see.'

'You caught him all right?'

'Yeah . . . 'e's quiet like. Not 'imself, see. Got 'im in the car.'

'That seems to be his usual place. His mobile kennel.'

'Tango likes the car, see.'

'Yes, I see.' It dawned on me why Ernie had offered to do a bit more work. He was worried about Tango and wanted me to look him over.

'We could finish the pipes in the bathroom,' offered Ernie.

'Thanks, but it's too late. My wife needs a rest.'

'Well, I been thinking. If you had a look at Tango . . . '

'If you're not happy about him, take him to his vet.'

'You're a vet, aren't yer?'

'Not Tango's. And I'm on vacation.'

'Yeah . . . Tango don't like 'is vet, see. It's a lady.'

'You could take him to Mr Brogan.'

'Dunno . . . 'e looks after cows.'

'He looks after dogs too.'

'Not greyhounds he don't.' Ernie shuffled his feet. 'Look 'ere, Mr Morton, Tango's racing Saturday week . . . '

'If that's the case you'd certainly be wise to take him to his vet.'

Ernie shook his head, dark eyes sorrowful. 'If Tango isn't right, I'll need to take a day off.'

'I wouldn't be surprised.' I was not going to be blackmailed.

'The guv'nor will send you another man . . . Stevie.'

'That's all right then.'

'Stevie's deaf.'

'It won't stop him working.'

'Naw. But Stevie got trouble with 'is back too, see. I mean, Stevie's okay. No one can say he ain't trying. But it's 'is back, see. It 'olds him up like. Stevie isn't a fast worker like me, see.'

Six

When Stevie failed to turn up in the morning Julia and I vacillated between frustration and relief. By eleven we'd sunk so low that the arrival of Ernie and Ferret sent us into a state of near-euphoria. No other state of mind would have induced me to ask Ernie how his greyhound was.

The expression in his eyes changed from surprise to hope. 'Tango's proper poorly . . . thanks for asking.'

'The vet's seen him?'

'Yeah. She's given 'im an injection of cortisone. Was that right?'

'I suppose so.'

'Mr Morton,' Ernie dropped the copperpipe he'd been about to cut. 'Tango don't like 'is vet.'

When I didn't respond he continued his work in aggressive slow motion. I had no wish to stay with the men, but I was certain that they needed supervision if we weren't to finish up with the lavatory overflow disgorging into the cavity wall. Oddly enough Ernie didn't seem to resent my advice and instructions.

At one point I asked him whether Mr Cobbler would be sending more men. 'It says in the specifications that all work was to be done by qualified craftsmen.'

'That's right,' agreed Ernie non-committally. 'Dunno whether the guv'nor's sending along anybody else.'

'It's a plumber who should be doing this pipe-work.'

'Yeah.'

'It shouldn't be you, anyway.'

'I'm doing it, ain't I?'

'It's wrong.'

'Why?' Ernie shrugged his massive shoulders. 'I'm a builder, ain't I?'

'A bricklayer.'

'Yeah.' Ernie gave an enigmatic smile, 'Building trade's depressed, see.'

After lunch a truck from Nether Craftly delivered our Buckingham Royal Thins. To me they looked exactly the same as the heating radiators we'd ordered in the first place. While Ernie and Ferret chucked the Buckingham Royal Thins into our front hall I checked the delivery note. Everything was there except the brackets, marked on the note with a question mark. The driver knew nothing about the brackets; either they were out of stock or it was up to Cobbler & Sons to supply something that would fix the radiators to the walls.

'You need special brackets for them radiators,' Ernie told me when the truck had left. 'I know. I fixed them Buckingham Royals over at the Manor House.'

'Then ask Mr Cobbler to get them.'

'Okay, if they're still in production. Trouble is, once they've stopped making them the suppliers run out of stock.'

After the exertion of unloading the radiators the men needed a prolonged rest. I left them asleep in the sun, Ernie's obscene belly rising above the food containers and thermos jars, and returned to cutting back the overhanging sycamore branches. It was the ideal occupation for working some of the frustrations of the building operations out of my system.

I'd been sawing away contentedly, enjoying the stillness

of the summer afternoon, when I became aware of plaintive sounds in Ernie's car. As I leaned into the Ford, Tango lifted his fine, narrow head, looked at me and made a soft crying noise in his throat.

'What's the trouble, boy?' I opened the back door and got in beside the greyhound. 'Haven't you had your walk?' I put the lead on him, but he wouldn't budge. He put down his head, making it clear that he didn't want out. 'Just bored?' Tango liked being stroked, but after a while he began to nudge my hand with his nose. He nudged until he had my hand on his right front paw. 'Hurting, is it?'

He let me take his paw and kept perfectly still while I examined it. I'd half expected to find a thorn or a wood-splinter in the pad or between the toes, but I found nothing. Automatically I continued the examination of the digits and the phalangal bones. As I felt around the second digit Tango jumped and gave a yelp of pain. 'You're a softy, Tango . . . it could be a knocked-up toe. But if it is, it's not bad.' I touched the same spot again, applying slightly more pressure. This time Tango didn't complain. 'There, you see. Bit of rest, that's all you need.'

As I got out of the car the dog followed me. I kept a firm grip on his collar. 'All right, let's see you walk.' I let go, hoping that he wouldn't fly off. He meandered to the nearest tree, lifted a leg and returned to the car. By then I had a good idea what was wrong with the dog. Not much. If he'd hurt a phalanx at all it was a very slight injury; on the other hand, I was sure that Tango had pulled a thigh muscle. Between the two things the dog was feeling sorry for himself, but neither injury would keep him off the race-track for long.

'Tango, you can tell the lazy sods who own you to take you for short, gentle walks . . . nothing strenuous for a day or two.'

'His vet said exercise 'im,' Ernie had done his walking-on-eggs thing and I hadn't heard him come up behind me.

'Same as usual says 'is vet . . . Mr Morton, what's it to be?'

'Whatever Tango's vet says.'

'Come on . . . you know more than what she does. Tango don't like 'er.'

'Ernie, I'm not taking your greyhound on.'

'Okay, okay. But we'll cut down 'is exercises, see.'

'Please yourself.'

'She wants to give 'im more injections. What about that then?'

'I've told you . . . '

Ernie turned towards the shed. 'You know them kitchen units you got?'

'Well?'

'The guv'nor can't get no 'inges for them, see.'

I was not going to be blackmailed into becoming Tango's vet. 'That's all right, I'll see to it myself.'

'Yeah? Well, you'll get no 'inges – not strong enough to take them heavy doors.'

'I suppose you could find us the right kind.'

'Maybe. Mate o' mine's got a business, see. Deals in accessories like.'

'I dare say he's expecting a delivery of all the things we need – including the brackets for the radiators.'

'That's right.'

'Good. You can bring them along tomorrow.'

'Naw, delivery'll be next week on account of the industrial dispute.'

'Does that mean a . . . night delivery next Wednesday? The kind that falls off the back of a lorry?'

'Depends . . . If them drivers's still in industrial dispute they won't go nowhere. But it'll be okay if they're just working to rule, see . . . What about them cortisone injections then?'

'Let me tell you something, Ernie. I don't care a damn about your mates' businesses, or parcels that fall off the backs of lorries, and . . . '

'But you care about Tango, don't you Mr Morton?'

He had me there, and he knew it.

'So what about them injections?'

What could I do? I liked that greyhound. 'If Tango were mine I wouldn't give him cortisone. But that's a personal opinion.'

'You got to be ethical like,' Ernie beamed, 'but I get you. About them 'inges and brackets . . . '

I remembered that it was Friday, the night when those mechanical monsters were due to defecate into the pit once again. 'Ernie, are you sure there won't be a delivery tonight?'

'Sure. Told you, didn't I? Them drivers is out on account of an industrial dispute. Next Wednesday they'll be working to rule . . . so you'll be okay for them bits you need.'

'Will it cost me extra?'

'Depends.'

'On what?'

'Well, we're in it together . . . me and me mates.'

Mike and Andy had come to inspect the building progress and noted how disappointing it was. They returned to the garden where I was setting up a barbecue.

'Where's mum?' asked Mike.

'Gone to the village.'

'Good.'

I knew exactly why he was glad to find her out. Because he was so close to his mother he had a good idea how she would be feeling, having to keep house in the shambles of our cottage. When Julia's temper was aroused Mike usually kept out of her way.

'Dad, I've had a letter from the DOE and . . . '

'What's that?'

'The Department of the Environment . . . about the natterjack toads. They do come under ESA,' he gave me his long-suffering look, 'the Endangered Species Act and the CWCA and . . . '

'Mike!'

'Okay, dad . . . the Conservation of Wild Creatures Act. So Andy and me and the FOE – the Friends of the Earth – can stop them tipping into the pit.'

'Mike, it's not that simple.'

'The letter says, we'll have official backing for any reasonable steps we take for the protection . . . '

'We are taking reasonable steps, Mike. We're trying to find out who's using the pit as a dump. With a bit of luck we'll know by next week.'

'Wish we'd know now . . . We've been asking everybody, and the FOE in Nether Craftly are on to it too, and we're putting up posters to tell people that the pit is an SSSI . . . all right dad . . . a Site of Special Scientific Interest.'

'Well, I hope you don't use all these initials on your posters or people won't know what you're talking about.'

'They can work it out,' said Andy.

'Not everyone's interested in your hobbies.'

'Wildlife isn't hobbies,' Andy rebuked me.

'No,' I admitted.

'This is hobbies.' Andy dipped a hand to the ground and performed a series of perfect cartwheels. Obviously Six's bionic-woman trainer was making something of the boys.

'Me too.' For a moment Mike put aside his zoological and academic interests and turned a neat somersault in mid-air. 'Inga's terrific.'

'So you're having a good time at the Habibs'.'

'Super. We're breeding fruitfly too.'

'And we've got tadpoles . . . Oh look!'

A 1945 Rover was coming down the drive and the boys raced off to meet it. My heart sank. There was only one pink Rover like it – my father-in-law's. If there was one person who wanted to see him even less than me, it was

Julia. She loved her father dearly; she just couldn't live with him for more than a couple of hours a month. Julia and the Colonel were so alike in temperament that they infuriated each other. In our present state of disorganization Colonel Jasper Hanley, ex-Indian Army, was about the worst visitor to happen to us.

As I watched him stalk towards me, tall and immaculately groomed in a cream shantung silk suit, my worst fears were confirmed. He was hugging a bottle of whisky, which meant that he'd come for the week-end or even longer. He always drank my whisky on shorter visits.

'There you are, old man,' he greeted me. 'Boys tell me you're in a proper mess . . . Never mind. Soon get things humming around here, I dare say. Took me three hours to get down here . . . blasted traffic. Can't imagine why people want to go rushing out of London like the Gadarene swine.'

'Well, you went rushing out of London.'

'Good reason. What? Make sure my girl's coping with life in the country and all that.'

'We're coping. But we won't be able to put you up, Jasper.'

'Rubbish. Boys are staying with friends, aren't they? Sleep in their room. Used to roughing it.'

'Not that rough.'

'Oh, I don't know. Stint I did at Ghazipur wasn't exactly a piece of cake. Under canvas. River flooded the camp. All hell let loose. Hundreds drowned. My batman was baling water all night long. Had a hell of a job keeping me dry.'

'Father-in-law, you haven't got a batman now and . . .'

'Julia will do.'

I was wondering whether there was any way of persuading the Colonel to stay at the Craftly Arms when Julia came driving up to the cottage. She saw the pink Rover, swerved wildly and almost crashed into the wall.

'Wow,' said Andy.

'FITF,' said Mike.

I had no trouble working that one out; *the fat's in the fire.*

Seven

My father-in-law turned down flat any idea of staying at the local pub. He didn't need looking after. He'd brew up for himself. He was well aware that Julia was congenitally incapable of letting any house guest fend for himself, but he wasn't going to worry about Julia's work-load or feelings.

After the Colonel had looked over the cottage the strangest thing happened. Julia, who'd learned early in life never to take her father into her confidence, opened her heart to him.

Out came her worries about the fact that Mr Cobbler still hadn't confirmed his estimate in writing, that Ernie was not a qualified plumber and Ferret no electrician, that Ernie's sledge-hammer was liable to break up more than the scheduled wall, damaging the very fabric of the ancient cottage. That Ernie and Ferret had been working slow-motion was self-evident.

'Loafing,' diagnosed the Colonel. 'Knew how to deal with that kind of thing in the army.'

'Daddy,' Julia looked alarmed. 'This isn't the army.' We were sitting at the table, a candle-lit island in the devastation of the kitchen. 'There are no more punka-wallahs. You can't order people around any more. If a man doesn't like the way you're treating him he just takes off and you're left with . . . well, a mess worse than this.'

'Rubbish, girl. Officer must have guts to command his men.'

'Daddy, Mr Cobbler's no officer.'

'Corporal-type, is he?'

'He's a smoothy who's trying to please everybody.'

'Never works. Now, don't you fret, girl. Haven't spent thirty years in the army for nothing.'

'Daddy . . . ' Julia's voice was weak. 'You're not going to . . . '

'What else? If there's one thing I can't stand it's seeing my family put upon.'

'We've been managing quite well . . . Really, daddy.'

'Got eyes in my head, haven't I? Chaps been playing you up. Soon get them sorted out.' The Colonel poured himself another whisky. 'When are they supposed to complete the job?'

'They won't make it.'

'Asked you a straight question. Expect a straight answer.'

'End of August,' said Julia, with uncharacteristic meekness. 'But it wouldn't be too bad if they finished by sixth of September.'

'They will.'

'Jasper,' I was appalled by father-in-law's unrealistic confidence. 'It's our architect's job to see the contract through and . . . '

'Met him, didn't I? When Constance wanted to buy this place . . . the estate-agent-Johnny.'

'It's his wife who's the estate agent.'

'So that's the set-up!' Evidently the Colonel was not uninformed about the ethics. 'Reckon Clive won't be much use to you. Slippery customer. But don't fret. Just leave it to me.'

'Daddy, one's got to be on the spot.' Julia played her last card. 'And you have to be in London.'

'What on earth for?'

'Constance . . . '

'Yes, Constance can look after my dog. Looked after hers often enough.'

This was one occasion when every word mattered. I was casting around for the right one. I couldn't appeal to the Colonel's protective instinct. He had none. He'd say that the lady he lived with was quite capable of taking care of herself. Besides – Constance, widow of Senator Pittsburgh, was cushioned by her butler and her money. Nor would she be bored without father-in-law; she was still busy writing the scandalous biography of her late husband, trying to create a posthumous Watergate-style sensation.

I said, 'You know, Constance is still an attractive woman.'

'Damned attractive,' agreed the Colonel. 'Wouldn't have bothered with her if she weren't.'

'You'd hate to lose her, wouldn't you?'

'My affair.' The Colonel calmly drained his tumbler and stuck out his aggressive Hanley chin. 'Going to keep Conny happy on week-ends. Quite enough for a woman her age.'

'But, daddy . . . '

'No buts, Julia. I intend to live in this cottage until I've licked your builder-chaps into shape.'

'Daddy, you simply don't understand . . . '

'That's enough from you, girl! More like your sainted mother every day; hell-cat with her equals, too soft with the servants.'

We were both on the job at seven-thirty on Monday morning; father-in-law standing over Ernie and Ferret, me watching father-in-law. The builders completed the plumbing and electrics in the bathroom and moved into the main bedroom. The Colonel, having inspected the work, fetched the men back into the bathroom.

'Left a couple of holes under the bath, didn't you?' observed the Colonel.

'Yeah,' agreed Ernie.

'Well, man, aren't you going to fill them up?'

'Naw. Them holes won't show when the panel goes back on.'

'Not good enough.'

Ernie's mouth fell open.

'Get your Tetrion – or whatever you've got for filling in holes, and finish the job.'

'Whatever for?'

'Because gaps like these are ideal nesting places for vermin.'

'Yeah?'

'Get a move on.'

To my amazement Ernie moved into the hall and returned with a carton of filler. He spent some ten minutes scrabbling behind the bath and when he came out the Colonel went down on the floor and inspected the job.

'Okay?' asked Ernie.

'Bit rough, but it'll do.'

Ernie looked relieved. 'The bath and them pipe's going to be boxed in, see.'

'Who's doing that?'

'Carpenter.'

'Should be done now. Must complete the bathroom. Where's the carpenter?'

'Well . . . ' the fat boy looked sheepish. 'We got a bit o' trouble at work, see. Our carpenters didn't turn up, on account of a grievance.'

'What the devil's that supposed to mean?'

'The guv'nor cut down their overtime, see. So they're 'aving an industrial *dis*pute.' Ernie pronounced dispute fashionably, with the stress on *dis*.

'Where do you come from?' asked the Colonel.

'Me?' Ernie went red in the face. 'Craftly born and bred, I am.'

'Then why don't you speak like an Englishman?'

'Sir?'

'In English we say dis*pute*.'

'Sorry, sir.' The fat boy looked ashamed of himself.

'Very well. I accept your apology. Now; where can I get hold of your best carpenter?'

'That's Dicky.'

'Well? I haven't got all day.'

'He's working at the vicarage, sir. He should be at work like. But he ain't, on account of the industrial dis . . . dispute, see.'

'So he's competing against his own boss?'

'Yeah.'

'Man should be sacked.'

'The guv'nor can't do it, sir . . . on account of *wrongful dismissal*. If 'e sacks Dicky, and Dicky takes him to the law, it'd cost the guv'nor a lot of time and money, see. Ain't worth it . . . not in a small firm like Cobblers, see.'

'That's blackmail. Right,' the Colonel dismissed Ernie with a flick of his hand. 'You can carry on in the bedroom now. I'll see to the carpenter.'

'Yes sir.'

At eleven o'clock I came to the conclusion that the new regime had been too good to last. Ernie, surrounded by his food-containers, went to lie in the sun; Ferret took Tango for a walk. The siesta had lasted for an hour when the Colonel came stalking into the garden.

'Mr Butters!' he trumpeted at Ernie.

'Sir!' The fat boy bounced to his feet with astonishing agility.

'Am I right in thinking that you're taking your elevenses?'

'Yes sir.'

'Then what the hell,' the Colonel's voice cut like ice into

the sunny day, 'what the hell are you doing here at twelve o'clock? The maximum for elevenses is ten minutes.'

'Yes sir.'

'Then see to it that it is no more than ten minutes in future, Butters.'

'Okay.'

'I beg your pardon Mr Butters?'

'I mean, yes sir.'

'Where's your man, Ferret.'

'Taking Tango for a walk . . . sir.'

'Who or what is Tango?'

'Our greyhound, like.'

'Exercising him in working hours, is he?'

'Well . . . I told 'im to, see.'

'You'd better make more suitable arrangements for Tango. This nonsense must stop.'

'Well sir, Tango's poorly, see.'

'What's the matter with the dog?' Father-in-law suddenly sounded human.

'Pulled a muscle in 'is thigh. Going after a rabbit's what's done it.'

'Don't you keep the dog in proper training kennels?'

'We do, sir. Tango was on holiday like when 'e did it. The vet would take 'im into hospital, but Tango don't like 'is vet, see.'

I thought it was time for me to intervene. 'Ernie's been trying to involve me . . . '

'I see,' father-in-law stopped me. 'We'll discuss this matter later. Mr Butters, today you'll let the dog out of the car within your proper rest periods . . . half an hour for lunch, fifteen minutes for tea. You'll make other arrangements for tomorrow. Dog shouldn't be in the car at all. Is that clear?'

'Sir . . . if I leave Tango at the vet's we – that's me and me mates – have to pay for it, see.'

'If you take the dog to work with you your employer

pays for it . . . because Mr Ferret doesn't have the time to put in an honest day's work. I call that stealing.'

Ernie looked as if he'd had his ears boxed. 'I got to think of Tango, sir.'

'You can leave the dog-problem to me. I'll see what I can do. Now, you've wasted enough working time; but if you stay on for an extra hour I'll say no more about it.'

At one o'clock father-in-law took off in his pink Rover. At two he returned, closely followed by Mr Cobbler and a lean, elderly man in a well-cut dark suit. The city-type turned out to be Dicky, the carpenter. The three of them, with me trailing behind, inspected the bathroom. Father-in-law and Mr Cobbler agreed that the carpenter should be starting his part of the job, and Cobbler took notes on the amounts of wood needed. Dicky, looking sour, showed some interest in the proceedings, which indicated that the *industrial dispute* had been settled.

'Any reason why the work on this floor shouldn't be completed by the end of this week?' the Colonel asked Mr Cobbler.

'No, there's no problem.'

'Except your workmen.' Father-in-law turned to me. 'I think I've convinced Mr Cobbler that he's going to lose money on this job unless he can get his men to earn their pay.'

'Yes . . . well . . . ' Dicky's presence seemed to embarrass Mr Cobbler. 'They're good men, Colonel.'

'Got to convince me.'

'There's the problem with Tango.'

'Know all about that.'

'It's Ernie, Colonel. He's a hard worker when he puts his mind to it, but he's sensitive.'

'Sensitive!' snorted the Colonel. 'What is he? An old woman?'

'Please!' Cobbler glanced nervously at Dicky. 'The situation is . . . '

'I won't have this word used in my presence.'

'Colonel?'

'*Situation*, man. Grossly overworked word. Mostly used without justification. Now, what are you trying to say? In proper English, if you please.'

'Er . . . Ernie's a good worker, basically. However, he does have the responsibility of the greyhound . . . which is owned by a syndicate of his – er – fellow workers and . . . '

'Including yourself, Cobbler?'

The builder gave a pink smile. 'As a matter of fact, I do have a small share in Tango. It's a matter of worker-management relations . . . '

'So you're not bothered about the dog.' The Colonel made it sound like a condemnation.

'I am . . . very concerned,' Cobbler assured him. 'But my prime consideration must be the fact that Tango's condition's affecting my best worker. While Tango isn't receiving the care Ernie feels the dog *should* have he won't put his mind to his work . . . I won't get the best out of Ernie; and I'm aware that I'm losing money because of this situa . . . state of affairs.'

'Ridiculous!'

'You don't race greyhounds, Colonel?'

'Certainly not. Wouldn't be seen dead at a greyhound stadium.'

'If you don't mind my saying so, sir, you're way out of date. There was a time – a good many years ago – when greyhound racing wasn't – er – socially acceptable. It was said to be rather crooked. But these days are past. I'd say there's no doping of dogs at all . . . probably due to the new scientific tests. It's a clean sport now, Colonel, and some of the best people go in for greyhound racing.'

'Such as?'

'The Duke of Edinburgh.'

'Don't believe it.'

'Absolutely true, Colonel. Though the Duke's dogs race in aid of a charity . . . the Playing Fields Association, I believe.'

'Ah,' the Colonel nodded, 'that's different. Polo-player myself. Duke plays a decent game too.'

Mr Cobbler was backing out of the bathroom. 'Well, I think we've got round our little problems . . . '

'We'll have got round them when the job's finished. Cobbler, from now on I'll expect you to show up here every day . . . and supervise your men.'

'Ernie's a good worker . . . '

'Sensitive, you said.'

'If we could get round Tango's little problem . . . '

'Told your man I'd look into it.'

'Colonel, there's a simple answer. I'm losing money on this job – as you've pointed out – and why? Because my best foreman's upset. Not to mince words, it's Mr Morton's fault.'

'You!' Father-in-law glared at me.

'This has nothing to do with me,' I protested.

'Mr Morton,' Cobbler spoke so softly that I felt like hitting him, 'I understand that Tango's really taken to you. And Ernie *has* asked you to look after him, hasn't he?'

'So that s it!' the Colonel turned to me. 'My son-in-law been making a mess of it, has he? Soon see about that!'

Eight

It wouldn't be a libel to say that the Colonel was an expert at using people for his own ends. Yet, in lifting our building work off the ground he had nothing to gain, on the face of it, unless it was the satisfaction of using his empire-building qualities, and possibly proving to us *youngsters* that we were weak and ineffectual. We'd be better at getting things done, he told us, if we didn't allow ourselves to get brain-washed by those sociology and trade union chaps. Our country was wilting away for lack of the charge-of-the-light-brigade spirit.

Within twenty-four hours of going into action the Colonel had certainly demonstrated that spirit. Though he hadn't quite created an army, he'd built himself the nucleus of a staff. Mr Cobbler, not so much a dodger as a non-decision maker, easily fell into a corporal-role. Ernie – who was capable of enterprise, on his own behalf at least – accepted the responsibilities and perks of a sergeant. Ferret remained what he was, a foot-slogging private, while Carpenter Dicky was regarded as a new recruit who'd have to serve his probation before getting appointed to the staff.

Dicky took advantage of the chink in the Colonel's armour – a total devotion to dogs – by wasting a whole morning on making a lattice-gate to fit across the doorway of our shed. The shed had been turned into a luxurious kennel for Tango, with a bed of straw plus our best blanket. The Colonel had told Julia to make her curtains elsewhere, and turned her out of the shed.

As it happened, Julia didn't get around to sewing curtains. Her father, who couldn't stand nibbling, was demanding *square* meals. He'd also given her the chore of taking Tango for frequent but non-strenuous walks. My job was to give Tango the required physiotherapy and keep Ernie happy in the belief that the dog would soon be fit for the race track again.

No doubt about it, father-in-law had turned the tables on me. The fact that the builders had been tinkering instead of working had been my fault, not theirs. I'd been guilty of a lack of leadership plus the inability to negotiate an effective alliance between the builders and ourselves. Had I responded to Tango's plight like a vet and a man, had I listened to Ernie's appeal, Operation Curate's Cottage would have been in full swing from the start.

Naturally father-in-law ignored my side of the story – that the men had gone slow even before Tango's accident, and that Ernie – far from appealing to me – had tried to blackmail me into accepting Tango as a patient.

No use crying over spilled milk: the Colonel had dismissed my objections. And so Tango came to live with us.

Streaky, who'd barked his head off when he'd discovered Tango on his territory, behaved with unexpected gentleness. While he'd never permitted healthy dogs, as distinct from bitches, into his home he had on occasions tolerated dog-patients of mine. Seeing me take Tango out of the Ford he watched, ears and one front paw lifted in concentration. Something in Tango's movements must have told our mongrel that the greyhound was below par. Streaky approached, tail wagging neither too slowly nor too enthusiastically, and cautiously touched noses with Tango. And Tango, friendlier and less sophisticated than our dog, responded with puppyish squeaks.

Throughout Tuesday and most of Wednesday the dogs remained in harmony, Streaky watched me work on Tango's thigh, Julia walked both of them, Ernie and his mates worked with a will and made visible progress.

Then, at three o'clock on Wednesday, the Colonel and I caught Dicky sneaking into his car.

'Where d'you think you're going?' asked father-in-law.

'I got to go to the bank.' Dicky, a dignified bean-pole in his city suit, started the engine. 'Bank shuts at three-thirty, see.'

'Taking time off in working hours.' There was menace in the Colonel's statement.

'I got to go to the bank on Mondays and Thursdays.'

'Today's Wednesday.'

'I missed Monday, see.'

The Colonel opened the car door on Dicky's side. 'On Fridays you finish work at three . . . which gives you a legitimate opportunity of visiting your bank. While you're working at Curate's Cottage, you'll be good enough to limit your bank-visits to Fridays between three-ten and three-thirty. Is that quite clear?'

Dicky had already switched off his engine. 'Yes, sir . . . But I've finished boxing in them pipes, see.'

'You telling me you've nothing to do?'

'S'right.'

'Then you'd better look again, man. Decent carpenter fills in on top of screw-heads . . . ready for priming and painting.'

'Painter's job,' grumbled Dicky.

'Not in my book.'

Dicky scowled. 'What're you on about? Is it a demarcation *dis*pute you're after?'

'The word – if you must use it – is dis*pute*. Stress on the second syllable.'

'Don't you play no games with me, mister!'

'Colonel to you. Now, see here . . . you'd better remember where I found you, if you know what's good for you.'

'I was in industrial dis . . . dis*pute* when I was doing the job in the vicarage,' Dicky tried to justify himself.

'Rubbish! It takes at least two people to start a dispute. You, my man, had not notified Mr Cobbler of your intention of stopping work. You just failed to turn up.'

'Mr Cobbler cut down me overtime.'

'Understand there was no need for overtime working.'

'Well, if a job don't get done . . . '

'Jobs didn't get done because you didn't put in a day's honest work. There'll be no more of that. Here, you damned well *will* earn your wages.'

'I can't knock meself out at work,' whined Dicky. 'Me and the wife can't manage without the overtime. We got our holidays to think about. Me and the wife's going on safari.'

'Safari?'

'Me and the wife's booked up for Kenya, see.'

'So you need the extra money,' said the Colonel, softly.

'You see the position, don't you sir?'

'Certainly do. But if you want to earn extra you'll put your back into it here . . . and do your bloody moonlighting at night.'

'I can't sir. I got a duodenal ulcer, see, and . . . '

'Ulcer, eh? Wouldn't go to Kenya if I were you.'

'Why's that then?'

'No hospitals in the bush. Ulcer perforates . . . you're a gonner.'

'I never thought of it . . . And we've booked . . . '

'What chaps like you need's a regular life . . . active day, sleep at night. Back to work, man! Chop, chop!'

The men had packed up for the day when Kath Greatorex came trotting up on a big chestnut hunter. Father-in-law, materializing from nowhere, helped her dismount. The tall horsewoman in black riding gear and bowler hat obviously enchanted him.

'Snifter?' he invited her.

Miss Greatorex looked at her watch. 'Nice idea. Thanks.'

The Colonel was conducting her to our table on the lawn. 'Always did admire a lady who looks at her watch before accepting a drink. Six o'clock . . . most civilized hour for a drink. In England, that is.'

'Brother was in the Guards,' volunteered Kath.

'Knew it from the way you sit your horse.'

Julia was sent for the whisky – ours, as the Colonel's bottle had been dead for some time – and Kath told father-in-law the tale of the sand-pit. By the end of the second snifter he had joined the Friends of the Earth and was planning the night's campaign against waste disposal. Kath mentioned that I hadn't allowed her to take the shotgun out of the car.

'Quite right,' said the Colonel.

Julia and I looked at one another, amazed that father-in-law appeared to be agreeing with me.

'Can have nasty accidents with shotguns,' he told Kath.

'Fair enough,' said Kath, amiably. 'With you in the party, Colonel, we'll manage without.'

'Tell you what,' the Colonel put his hand over Kath's. 'No reason why I shouldn't bring my own rifle.'

'No hardware,' I told him.

'Not asking you to join us, Michael. Got a greyhound to look after. Better stick to your own trade.'

It didn't surprise us that Kath Greatorex invited the Colonel to dinner and suggested that he should accompany her to the sand-pit in her car. His tactics with women – with the exception of his daughter and late wife – had always been remarkably effective. Julia and I, happy to be on our own, dined on sausages and mash and then started on decorating the bathroom. As experienced painters and paper-hangers we were going to do the whole cottage ourselves.

Shortly before midnight I went off to the sand-pit. This time the sky was clear and the light of an almost full moon made the going easy. The Colonel and Kath Greatorex were there already, the boys' bionic-woman trainer arrived on the stroke of twelve. The Colonel, presumably in memory of nights on patrol, had brought his hefty leather-covered hip-flask and was passing it around. Inga refused, on the grounds that alcohol made one's brain-cells die, but the rest of us took quite a few swigs. By the time the two juggernauts appeared I felt more like a party-goer than a conservationist.

The two big transports stopped at the edge of the pit. I was expecting the articulated containers to rise and disgorge their noxious cargo when the drivers' doors opened and two men came dropping to the ground. As they lit one another's cigars I could see that they were quite young. We advanced on them, Kath in the lead.

'Friends of the Earth,' she snapped at the young men.

'Hello,' the taller of them greeted us. 'My friend's Fitzroy Spassky and I am Augustus Park-Burnend.'

The cultured voice had a damping effect on us all. For what seemed ten minutes or more the only audible sound was the croaking of frogs.

'Natterjack,' said Kath, at last.

'An unusual toad, I believe,' said Augustus. 'How interesting. . . . Of course, that explains why you're here. Friends of the Earth . . . conservationists.'

'Exactly,' said Kath. 'Terrifically bucked that natterjacks have come to live here. Got to stop tipping rubbish at once.'

'You're absolutely right.' Augustus emitted a cloud of fragrant smoke. 'Cigar?'

'No thanks.'

'Smells pretty good,' said the Colonel.

'Oh, they're marvellous cigars,' agreed Augustus. 'My old man has them sent directly from Havannah.' He offered a silver case, and the Colonel accepted them.

'Jasper,' Kath rebuked him, 'Think we should get down to business.'

'Quite agree m'dear . . . Mr – er – Augustus, you going to tip all this rubbish into the pit?'

'No, as a matter of fact.'

'Did you dump waste last week?' I asked.

'Yes, as a matter of fact.'

'Your containers can't be empty tonight,' suggested Kath.

'They aren't. But we have no intention of discharging the loads.'

'Can't make head or tail of it,' complained father-in-law.

'Actually it's quite simple,' Agustus assured him. 'We should have done a trip last Friday, but we were in industrial dispute . . .'

'Pronouncing it properly anyway,' muttered the Colonel.

'In industrial dispute with our employers. As a result we didn't undertake any night-journeys.'

'What were your grievances?' The Colonel glanced at Kath, assuring himself that she appreciated his knowledge of modern industrial relations.

'Actually there are two issues; single-man manning . . . driving long distances on your own can become frightfully boring. Fitzroy and I always had mates in the cabs until the administration decided to cut the cost of waste-disposal. That's how the dispute began. Naturally that phase couldn't last . . . people get frightfully uptight when the refuse piles up on their doorsteps. Hence the admin people offered to enter negotiations, provided we resumed the trips . . . That's why we're here tonight.'

'But you're not going to dump the waste?' asked Kath.

'No. You see, we've progressed from industrial dispute procedure to working-to-rule. Under work-to-rule we are obliged to travel to the tips . . . but there's nothing in the regulations that requires us to discharge our loads. We've notified admin that we'll continue our work-to-rule until our second grievance has been dealt with . . . to our satisfaction.'

'Money,' said Inga feelingly.

'Absolutely,' agreed Augustus. 'We're claiming hostility money, and we consider that we have an excellent case.'

'Heard of dirty money,' said the Colonel, 'sewage chaps entitled to it. Get mucky, you know.'

'Hostility money's based on psychological stress,' explained Augustus. 'The nuclear fuel workers got it first, because their industry's frightfully unpopular. They have rather a thin time with women; girls are scared of becoming radio-active. We waste disposal officers feel that we're in an equally unsocial industry . . . You've no idea how rude people can get when they catch us dumping in their neighbourhood.'

'Okay for you, Gussy,' the second driver chipped in. 'He can smarm 'is way out of trouble on account of 'im being an educated bloke. 'E's got a degree from the Limehouse School of Economics and Sociology,' Fitzroy told us, proudly. 'He's our shop-steward.'

'Shop-steward,' barked the Colonel, 'should be ashamed of yourself, man.'

'It's a case of swings and roundabouts,' sighed Augustus. 'Death duties, imposed by the government, absolutely beggared my family. I've got to claw back some of our money if the Park-Burnend clan's to survive in *some* sort of style.'

'With you now,' said the Colonel. 'Well done . . . Snifter?' He passed the hip-flask to Augustus.

'Thank you, sir. I won't if you don't mind. I never drink when I'm driving. Actually, I think principles are frightfully out-of-date; but I decided to adopt this one principle for tradition's sake.'

The Colonel took back the hip-flask and poured whisky down his gullet. 'Good man . . . Now, what's the next move? Accept that you won't be dumping tonight. What about your next trip?'

'I expect it'll be the same . . . with the same refuse in our containers. The hostility-money issue won't be solved for some time . . . chiefly because the principle of it is rather new.'

'What'll happen to the refuse?'

'We hate inconveniencing the public . . . but I'm afraid the rubbish will just accumulate on people's doorsteps.' Augustus ground his cigar-stub into the grass. 'Time to go back, Fitzroy.'

'Righto.'

'Wait,' I stopped the men. 'Where's the parcel?'

'What parcel?' Fitzroy eyed me suspiciously.

'Mate of mine asked me to pick it up. Ernie Butters. There should be hinges for kitchen cupboards and brackets for radiators.'

'Right,' Fitzroy sounded convinced. 'Get it for you.'

When he gave me the package I felt I'd shut the stable door after the horse had bolted. Ernie, thanks to father-in-law, *had* succeeded in making me treat his greyhound. The only satisfaction in hijacking the parcel was that Ernie would be inhibited in extorting money for the contents. Those hinges and brackets *wouldn't* cost me extra, whoever Ernie's mates and business associates were.

The drivers had climbed back into their cabs when I

remembered to examine the transports. On the off-side I found an elegant coat of arms and - in gold letters – *Havantshire County Council.*

I swung myself up to Augustus's level. 'You're taking rubbish all the way from Havantshire?' I asked.

'We are, actually.'

'All this distance?' It seemed hard to believe.

'This is one of our shorter runs . . . Some of us go up as far as Cumberland.'

'That's mad. Why not dump the rubbish in your own county.'

'As a matter of fact that *is* the policy the administration's tried to implement for a long time. But we're resisting it.'

'Why? Surely it's sensible.'

'In industry one can't afford sensible policies. If the waste disposal officers allowed local authorities to dump refuse in their own counties a lot of men would be laid off. There'd be a rise in unemployment.'

'Surely it wouldn't affect many people and . . . '

'You'd be surprised,' said Augustus. 'It's a nation wide problem . . . affecting thousands of waste disposal officers. Especially drivers and their mates.'

'You don't mean . . . '

'Of course. Somerset dumps in Havantshire . . . Havantshire dumps in Surrey . . . your County might be sending its waste to Scotland – for all I know.'

'It's shunted all over the country!'

'Wherever we can find suitable dumps. Provided we stand up for ourselves and remain militant, ours is one of the few growth-industries in the country.'

It was after one in the morning when Kath Greatorex dropped us at the gates to the vicarage and Curate's Cottage, yet the groundfloor of the vicarage was still brightly lit.

'Going in.' The Colonel made for the path to the big house.

I gripped his arm. 'Not now.'

'Want to end rubbish-tipping. Chap owns the pit, doesn't he?'

'Yes. But we're not going to do anything in the middle of the night.'

'Chap's not in bed yet.'

'Never mind.'

'Trouble with you . . . letting things slide,' groused the Colonel. But he followed me to the archway leading to our drive.

An owl, looking like a pale ghost in the moonlight, came fluttering from the stable block. A brilliant pair of eyes, cat or fox, flashed past and disappeared in the bushes. I recognized the honey-scent that reached us in small wavelets, and made a mental note to plant a buddleia next year. The boys would enjoy identifying and watching the butterflies which buddleia attracted.

'Got to act, y'know,' said father-in-law.

'I'll go and see Choy tomorrow.'

'Lunch-time. Got to watch those chaps of yours.'

'Morning,' I told him. 'I won't need you at the vicarage.'

'Reckon you will. Experience with Chinese, don't you know.'

'Peking Chinese perhaps; not Huddersfield or Glasgow Chinese.'

'Think Choy's born and bred in UK?' asked the Colonel, thoughtfully.

'I shouldn't be surprised. In any case, I'm going to handle the Choys my way. They happen to be our nearest neighbours. So keep out of it.'

We'd come level with the front entrance of the vicarage when the whole building seemed to explode into a mass of lurid lights. A long, loud scream shattered the stillness of the night.

Nine

There'd been an explanation for the outburst we'd seen and heard at the vicarage. A couple of vans, parked at the side of the house, had made it clear that *experts* had been testing the kind of mobile light-effects that go with stereo equipment and pop music. No doubt they'd been moonlighters. By day the vicarage tended to be so quiet that it seemed uninhabited.

Walking through the beautiful grounds, once owned by the Church, it occurred to me that we'd probably taken a very unfair view of our builders. For all I knew they were the hardest working men in the European Economic Community, working for a building or electrical firm by day – at least to a degree which preserved them from getting tired – and earned themselves a second lot of wages by night.

As the bell at the front didn't seem to be functioning I went to the back of the vicarage. I hadn't seen it since we'd looked at Curate's Cottage for the first time and decided to buy it. The change was amazing. The old kitchen garden and shrubbery had been made into a big car park, and a wide road had been cut through the trees. I recalled that there had been a parcel of land for sale between the church and the recreation ground. The Choys must have acquired it for the purpose of making a new approach to their country club. As a result of the new lay-out the back of the vicarage looked like a stately home. Only one thing spoiled the impression; the much enlarged doorway was framed in white-painted panels full of capital letters.

The top one read, SIMPKINS-CHOY'S HEALTH AND COUNTRY GLUB. The right-hand panel announced, in smaller letters, VERY SPORTING FACILEMENTS. EVEN ETHICAL AND ETHNIC MASSAGES. CLIENTS' BIORHYTHMS DIAGNOSED AND ELECTRONICALLY TRIPAL CHEQUED FOR GIVING OUR CLIENTS FINE EXPLOITMENT OF THEIR OWN TOP-ENERGETICS. ALSO HAIR AND BEATYFICATION TREATMENTS.

The writing in the left-hand panel was interspersed with slits, push-buttons and steel-framed glass flaps roughly eight inches square. The top part said, CHINESE DRIVE-AWAY DINNERS, FROM RECEIPES CREATED BY BUDDHIST MONKESSES TRAINED IN THE MYSTERIOUS EASTEND. The rest were instructions on how to get the drive-away dinners out of the automat. POST £2 IN SLOT, OBTAIN HOT DRIVE AWAY DINNER FROM FOR-ONE CUBBYHOLE. POST £4 IN SLOT, OBTAIN HOT DRIVE-AWAY DINNER FROM FOR-TWO CUBBYHOLE. REPEAT MULTIPLICITIES FOR LOTS OF EATERS.

I was standing there, wondering how the village of Craftly would respond to such enterprise, when Mr Choy appeared on his doorstep. He pressed his palms together and bowed Chinese fashion. When he recognized me a smile came into his dark eyes, the arms dropped to his side. 'Nice to see you,' he greeted me. His Scottish accent was slight; more of an intonation. 'My wife and I thought of calling in at your cottage, but I thought ye'd be too busy for visitors . . . Come in, Mr Morton.'

He led me into a big reception hall with deep blue walls,

white paintwork and comfortable leather armchairs. 'Would ye like some tea?'

I thanked him and said that I couldn't stay long.

'Aye, workmen keep one busy. What do you think of the old vicarage now?'

'Quite a change.'

'Shows you what can be done with a bit of imagination.'

'It'll be quite a business.'

'Yes, we hope it will.'

'You've lived in the country before?'

'Best part of my life. The family home's near Pitlochry . . . Originally we're from Hongkong, but I'm a second generation Scot.'

'But the notices outside . . . '

Choy's face remained immobile, but his eyes were laughing. 'Pidgin English? Well, it's what our clients would expect. You know, the mysterious East and all that. It would be a shame to disappoint them.'

'What do you mean by *biorhythms?*'

'It's a matter of cycles. All people have a 23-day physical cycle, a 28-day emotional and a 33-day intellectual cycle. There's a new electronic calculator out – from America of course – that can tell anyone his high and low. You just feed in your birth-date and the calculator tells you when you're at your best or your worst . . . It could help you plan your work and your leisure so you know when to get most enjoyment from your activities. Would you like me to demonstrate the machine?'

'Perhaps another time, Mr Choy.'

'My name's Malcolm . . . Yours is Michael, I believe.'

'Yes . . . Well, I'd like to know what you're planning to do with the sand-pit. I imagine you wouldn't like to have a rubbish-tip at the back of this fine place.'

'That arrangement goes back to when my father-in-law owned the pit.'

'It's still in force?'

'Only until the end of the month. I've notified Havantshire County Council that I'm not renewing the contract . . . It's worked out very well; the tipping's saved us a lot of in-filling.'

For a moment it had sounded easy; no more waste-disposal at the back of the cottage; instead, golfers on a well-kept green. Then it hit me. Malcolm Choy's plans for the sand-pit – much as I liked them – were bound to run into trouble. As soon as I heard the doorbell I knew that trouble had arrived.

The Colonel had introduced himself as a member of Friends of the Earth and told Choy, in his usual abbreviated manner, that the sand-pit – as an abode of the natterjack – was a place to be protected from County Councils by its owner.

'No allowy throwy nasty thingy in,' the Colonel wound up in a travesty of pidgin English.

'You've spent your life in China?' asked Choy, politely.

'What's that?'

'In an English colony, of course.'

'Don't know what you mean.'

'Your English, sir . . . ' Choy couldn't quite hide his amusement. 'It's a bit shaky. But I'm sure it'll improve if you stay in Craftly for a while. It's a pleasant village; people are not unsympathetic to colonials.'

'Now look here . . . ' The Colonel's face had gone red. 'I know you lot eat frog's legs and . . . '

'The French do, I believe.'

'And birds' nests . . . '

'Not English birds' nests, they'd be too tough.'

'I haven't come here to argue with you about . . . '

Choy put the palms of his hands together and bowed. 'I wouldna arrgue with a guest,' he said in his best Scottish accent, 'especially when we share similar interrests.'

'Eh?'

'I'm a founder member of the Craftly branch of the Friends of the Earth, Colonel. So far, I'll readily admit, I've been too busy to attend the meetings . . . busy dealing with the pollution of the river and the Craftly dewponds. So I'm most grateful to you for bringing the plight of the natterjack toads to my attention.'

The Colonel knew he'd been up-staged, but he wasn't beaten. 'What are you going to do to preserve the toad's habitat?'

'I think I'll phone my cousin in the States.'

'Don't know what you're talking about.'

'Lou Choy's a professor at UCLA.'

'Eh?'

'The University of California at Los Angeles.'

'Nothing to do with the subject.'

'Colonel, it has everything to do with the subject. My cousin is one of the world's experts on toads. He'll be most interested in the appearance of natterjacks on my property, and I wouldn't be surprised if he flew over to see them.'

'Bonkers if he did.'

'Not at all. American universities are generous in paying research expenses, especially when it concerns conservation.'

'Won't get us anywhere.'

'We'll get expert advice,' I chipped in.

'That's right,' agreed Choy. 'And it goes without saying that I'll abide by my cousin's advice . . . and recommendations.'

'Well,' the Colonel got up, 'need to discuss it with Kath Greatorex. Don't you think, Michael?'

I said, 'You can visit Kath without talking toads.'

Choy looked from one to the other of us. 'You've met before?'

'We're giving him a bed at the moment,' I told him. 'When one's got to deal with moonlighting builders, old colonials like him earn their keep.'

'Michael,' hissed the Colonel, 'I'll have your hide for this.'

'It won't do, father-in-law. Remember, you joined the Friends of the Earth . . . Yesterday, was it?'

I heard the crash long before our cottage came into view. Ernie's sledge-hammer? But the men hadn't yet finished the plumbing and wiring. Besides we had agreed – or so I thought – that Ernie would finish demolishing the wall by a less brutal method.

Outside the cottage Ernie and Ferret were sitting under a tree, surrounded by sandwich boxes and beer cans. The Colonel, still licking the wounds he'd received at the vicarage, chose to ignore them and made himself scarce.

At our open door the sunlight was full of dust-particles. I went in search of Julia and eventually found her in the living room, screw-driver in hand, in a state of shock.

I put an arm around her. 'What's the matter, love?'

'Look.' She put her head on my shoulder and burst into tears.

I became aware of an appalling sight – a still-life of violence. At one stage in the cottage's history, probably in the Victorian era, someone had bricked up the big inglenook fireplace – to save fuel, presumably – and set in an ugly little coal-fire contraption. We had instructed our architect and builders to remove it and to restore the inglenook to its original state. Ernie had knocked out the brick-front all right – with the sledge-hammer – but in the process he'd opened up a wide crack in the chimney.

'It'll never work now,' Julia sobbed, her dream of Christmas log-fires shattered. 'And they . . . promised to use a hammer and chisel.'

'We're not going to pay Cobbler until they've repaired this damage.'

'They'll say . . . that it *was* like this.'

'They won't get away with it. It's perfectly obvious that it's a new crack.'

Julia dried her eyes with the back of her hand, making a black smear across her forehead. 'Michael, is there any hope of getting it repaired?'

'It will be,' I promised her grimly. 'What are you doing with the screw-driver?'

She pointed, silently. There was a pick-axe lying by the window. Our fine old oak-floor had clearly been assaulted with it, one of the strips splintered and chewed up beyond repair. 'Is that how they were going to lift the floor-boards?'

Julia nodded. 'I caught them . . . but not in time.'

'Only one board gone. It could have been worse.'

'Michael, I lost my temper with them. I . . . I offended them.'

'Good. What did you do?'

'I called them vandals . . . And I made them watch me lift a floor-board with the screw-driver. Ernie didn't like it.'

'So what!'

'He said, if I was so good at it why didn't I do the job myself . . . Then they walked out on me.'

'Well, they haven't gone home.'

'But Ernie said they weren't going to touch another thing in the cottage . . . they'll wait for Mr Cobbler. And Mr Cobbler's in Cornwall.'

Ten

For the rest of the working week Ernie and Ferret sunbathed and consumed vast quantities of food and beer. Dicky didn't show up at all. Father-in-law, taking pleasure in demonstrating that we weren't getting anywhere with the builders without his whip-cracking, took himself off. We knew he wouldn't be at a loss, not with a woman on his hook and a good pub in the neighbourhood.

At five minutes to three, on Friday, Ernie and Ferret were ready to take off for the weekend. I was at the bedroom window, painting the frame, when Ernie came strolling along and looked up. 'How's it going then?'

'Very well. This room and the bathroom will be finished by Monday I expect.'

'I mean . . . Tango.'

'You're right. Better take him with you.'

''E's okay then?'

'He isn't fit for the race-track yet, if that's what you mean. But I don't want to keep him.'

'You're his vet,' said Ernie accusingly. 'I mean, he needs 'is treatment, don't he? You said you was going to look after 'im.'

'That was when you were working for us.'

'Working now, ain't we?'

'I thought you were on strike.'

'Industrial action?' he sounded shocked. 'No, we're not involved in no industrial action. Not us.'

'So what *have* you been doing the last couple of days?'

'Well, we just took time off for consultation, see.'

'And what conclusion did you arrive at?'

'We got to see the guv'nor. We need the electric cutter, see . . . for taking down the wall.'

'Is it under Mr Cobbler's bed?'

'It's not the cutter, see. It's the wiring. Got to get the Inspector from the Electricity Board. 'E's got to test the circuits, see.'

'You mean . . . before you use electrical equipment you want to make sure that you don't blow yourself up.'

'Stands to reason, don't it? Got to get the guv'nor to get the Inspector.'

'I expect that'll take time, so you'd better take Tango with you.'

'Get the Inspector here first thing Monday morning . . . Mr Morton, you wouldn't take it out on a dog what's poorly, would you?'

'Take what out?'

'Well . . . I mean to say, there's been hold-ups like. You got to expect it . . . About them hinges for the kitchen units, there's been an 'old-up too. They was supposed to arrive . . . '

'I know.'

'I can't 'elp it, see. They was supposed to deliver them. I'll get on to me mate. If you keep Tango . . . for 'is treatment like . . . '

'I will, if you come in tomorrow morning and fix the radiators for us.'

'Can't; not without them brackets.'

'I've got brackets.'

'Yeah? Tomorrow's Saturday.'

'Well?'

'You mean, do the job for you private like?'

'I mean, just do the job.'

'On a Saturday? That'll cost you extra.'

'I might give you a discount.'

'What on? I'm not buying nothing from you.'

'Oh yes, you are . . . my professional services.'

Fat boy looked alarmed. 'You aren't giving me no vet bill, are you?'

'I'm sure Tango's former veterinary surgeon didn't treat him for nothing.'

'That's different, see. I mean, you do things for your mates, don't you? If I fix your radiators on a Saturday . . . '

'I wouldn't want you to, except on a business basis.'

'I dunno . . . ' Ernie pushed up his woolly hat and scratched underneath. 'I got the guv'nor to think of.'

'Thoughtful of you. I'll tell him you came in on Saturday to make up for time you lost on Thursday and Friday.'

'Can't do that!' Ernie looked shocked. 'I mean, I'd get in trouble with the Union. Making up for lost time . . . that's a black-leg situation. Get it?'

I said, 'Let's forget the whole thing, shall we? I'll be too busy to look after your dog. Take him away.'

'Didn't say I wasn't coming, private like. Now did I?'

I dipped my brush into the paint and got on with the job.

'Listen,' pleaded Ernie, down below. 'Saturdays I like to lie in, see. Eight-thirty okay with you?'

'Suit yourself.' I was wondering whether I was pursuing the right *labour relations* policy. Ernie, probably because he'd heard me talk to his dog, had made up his mind that I was the right vet for Tango. Clearly, Tango was important enough for him to put himself at a disadvantage in his dealings with me. Not having worked on a basis of mutual blackmail before, I couldn't tell whether the results would justify such a contest.

Ernie shuffled his feet. 'See you in the morning then . . . And about them brackets. You sure you've got the right size?'

'Yes.'

'Where did you get 'em, then?'

'From a mate of yours.'

At tea-time Mike and Andy came visiting us. I told them the good news that the home of the toads was safe. Mike immediately pointed out that it wouldn't remain safe once Mr Choy went ahead with the development of a golf course. Mike had been planning ahead. He'd telephoned the well-known TV naturalist, Archie Bell, who had given him information and advice.

The boys had been concerned because they'd been unable to find the natterjacks. Mr Bell had explained to them that the toads disliked extremes of temperature and had almost certainly stayed in their burrows on account of the drought.

'Our tadpoles are becoming natterjacks too,' said Andy. 'So Mike asked Mr Bell what we're to do with them.'

Tea in the garden on a hot summer's day, the children chattering away, Julia looking tremendous in a yellow bikini . . . it was a foretaste of summers to come, when the cottage would be comfortable and the cakes home-made.

Mike helped himself to another rock bun. He didn't seem to mind that it had come out of a plastic packet. 'Natterjacks go looking for water,' he said, 'because they need the right kind of pond to breed in. They lay thousands of eggs in two long jelly tubes and then the tadpoles jump out and . . .'

'And little boys,' Julia smiled, 'who should know better, catch them and put them in glass jars.'

'Mr Bell said he was glad we did 'cause it's a special toad and it might die out. So he told us how to look after the tadpoles . . . and he's coming to see them . . . and he said we should put the young toads into a vivarium . . . and Sheik Habib's getting us a vivarium . . .'

'How's Sandy?' I asked.

'He's all right,' Mike told us. 'But we haven't found any more sand lizards, so Mr Bell's going to take him away 'cause he knows a place where there are more lizards like him . . . Dad, can we take Tango for a walk?'

'He's been out enough today.'

'Can we give him physio?' asked Andy.

We let the greyhound out of the shed and he lay down on the lawn, showing pleased anticipation. Having his front end caressed by the boys and the rear end massaged by me was his idea of the good life. Tango had been racing since the age of fifteen months and he was almost four years old now. In a year or eighteen months his track career would be over and I wondered whether Ernie would keep him on as a pet. Did Ernie care about the dog because he won races or because he was a nice, gentle character?

'What's going to become of him?' asked Julia, picking up my thoughts – not for the first time. She too had become fond of Tango.

'I'll keep an eye on him.'

'Do you think Ernie will want you to remain his vet?'

'Yes . . . if I charge him less than the woman vet. And Julia, you can't have him.'

'When he retires from racing . . . '

'A greyhound in London's out of the question.'

'Claire and Tiger've got a retired greyhound,' said Andy.

'That's right.' Mike scratched Tango under the chin, which made the hound grin. 'You'll see him tonight . . . Claire said, will you and mum go over to dinner with them. They've found a new sort of frozen fish from Russia in the supermarket . . . and they want to try it out on you. And Claire wants you to come 'cause Tiger's had a disaster.'

Eleven

It was Claire and Tiger's lifestyle rather than their cooking that always made us look forward to their dinners. Claire's lilac-pointed Siamese cats had been among the first patients I'd treated when I'd started practising in Knightsbridge. In each Siamese generation there had been at least one kitten that grew up to spend its days around Claire's neck, draped like those fox-collars worn by my mother's generation.

We'd known Claire and her cats in her bachelor-girl London flat, with its walls in lilac and yellow stripes and black ceilings with white footprints. In those days she'd worked in Tiger's antique business as an interior decorator. When Tiger had inherited the title Lord St George Clemens they'd married and taken their violent colour-schemes to Craftly Manor, furnishing the vast house with American antiques. Tiger's success as a playwright had made large-scale house-keeping impractical – the St George Clemenses had to spend a lot of time abroad – and so they'd sold the Manor House to Sheik Ahmed Habib. Their new residence in the grounds of the Manor, called 2001, looked like a flying saucer from outside. Inside, the black ceilings were curved in army-hut style and the walls – either lilac or mustard yellow – were decorated with posters of Tiger's Broadway and London plays.

Julia and I walked across Farmer Thornton's land and were approaching 2001 by a path leading through the orchard when Julia abruptly stopped.

'Michael, *somebody* actually built this flying saucer.'

'Obviously.'

'Just think! It means there's somebody, somewhere who's capable of building . . . not just an ordinary house, but an unusual one. Do you realize what it means?'

'That we might have found better builders than ours. But it's too late to change. We can't afford to pay twice for the same job.'

'Wish we'd asked Tiger's advice when we bought the cottage.'

'He might have employed flying saucer specialists, twice as expensive as our lot. Julia – just for the one evening – let's forget about builders.'

We were making for the arched front door when we heard screams that made me shiver – they were so dismal and pained. My first thought was that Claire had told Tiger that she didn't like his latest play – an almost unthinkable reaction from her – and that Tiger was pursuing her with a hatchet. But then Tiger was much too mild and well-mannered for such an outburst of temperament. Besides, the screams were coming from somewhere above us.

Suddenly we saw them – a couple of pure white peacocks, their tails as delicate as Nottingham lace. They were sitting in the branches of an apple tree, screeching at the setting sun.

Claire opened the door and swept us into her arms. 'Darlings! how lovely to see you! Did Anthony one and two scare you? We have two Anthonies and one Cleopatra . . . I don't see why not; as Tiger said, Cleopatra did have more than one man in her life. Aren't they gorgeous birds! And they're better at telling us when someone's coming to see us than Andromeda.'

As we stepped into the hall a big greyhound came rushing at me. Leaping on her hindlegs, she put her paws on my shoulder and wiped her tongue across my face.

'Down Meda!' ordered Claire. Not trusting the bitch's obedience, she grabbed Andromeda by the collar and dragged her off me. 'Meda's usually quite good, but she's on heat just now.' She adjusted the Siamese cat on her neck. 'Chang-Ching doesn't like it one bit . . . She's more nervous than the cats we had in London. Do you remember them?'

'Chou-en-Lai and Mao-tse-Tung,' said Julia. 'I've never forgotten them.'

'Chang-Ching's called after the widow of Mao-tse-Tung . . . We thought we'd like to keep a family continuity . . . She's a darling, really; but a bit difficult with Meda at the moment, but absolutely marvellous with the peacocks. Come in. We're in the kitchen. Tiger's found a Russian fish, frozen of course, in Nether Craftly super market and he's doing his chef thing . . . you know, working out a super sauce.'

The kitchen was exactly what Julia wanted in our cottage. It was large, lined with natural wood cupboards and festooned with strings of onions, garlic and bunches of herbs. On the massive pine table in the centre stood raffia-covered wine bottles and candles in polished brass holders.

'Don't mind eating in the kitchen?' Tiger greeted us. He was wearing a white-striped blue butcher's apron and a chef's hat which made him look about seven feet tall. 'Got to watch the sauce. I rather think it might curdle if it doesn't go straight from the cooker to the table.'

'The kitchen's lovely,' Julia assured him.

Claire, without asking what we wanted, gave us big slugs of vodka. 'We brought it back from Russia.'

'When were you there?'

'In March and April . . . Easter. They put on Tiger's play

Psht. Do you know, it was the wildest success ever. Better than in the States. One of the interpreters told us that the Moscow churches were half empty for the first time in years . . . because people went to *Psht* instead.'

'Not necessarily true,' growled Tiger.

'Darling. I'm sure it was . . . You see, *Psht* was so absolutely right for the Russians. It was *the* play that Tiger didn't write. He *created* it, in sort of lines on graph-paper. *Psht* really is the ultimate in non-communication . . . so you can imagine why it appealed to the Russians. You know that wonderful scene when Walter steps over Marian – Marian's lying on the floor – when he steps right over her and turns off the television set . . . The audience was in tears!'

'Well . . . ' Tiger, stirring the sauce on the cooker, kept his eyes modestly on the job in hand. 'It's easily the best scene I ever created.'

'One of the best,' protested Claire. 'I think the bicycle scene in *Three Brassieres to Bond Street* was fabulous. And the opening of *Three Corsets to Curzon Street* . . . the *New York Times* critic wrote that the play had all the qualities of a Shakespeare drama, except that Shakespeare needed words and Tiger doesn't.'

'Claire, darling, do stop it,' said Tiger.

Coming from him, the objection was truly startling. I remembered Mike's remark that Tiger'd had a *catastrophe*. Had someone, after all those rave notices, given him a bad write-up? He'd take it hard. Behind his rugged ginger exterior Tiger was not insensitive.

'Shall I serve the fish?' asked Claire meekly.

'Aren't we having starters?'

'Oh, darling!' wailed Claire. 'I'm sorry. I should have de-frosted the sweet corn.'

'How about some caviar?'

'All gone, darling. The cats absolutely adored it.'

The cat did not adore the defrozen Russian fish – a coarse-grained monster with an unpleasant smirk on its face, which proved hard to swallow despite the curdled cream-sauce that was meant to help it down one's gullet. The Siamese, descending Claire's shoulder with slow grace, landed on the dinner table. She cautiously approached the fish, put out a paw, and whipped off a morsel. One sniff was enough for Chang-Ching. Abandoning the titbit she leaped back on the shoulder and vigorously washed the paw which had been in contact with the Russian fish.

'What do you think of it?' Tiger asked Claire.

'Well darling . . . it's got an interesting texture.'

Tiger swallowed hard. 'Dare say it's too ethnic for western tastes . . . too Slavonic.' He turned to Julia, 'To my mind there's a crucial difference between us and the Russians. Give you an example. Take a roomful of comfortable armchairs with a single uncomfortable wooden one among them. Any of *us* would choose an armchair to sit in, but a Russian entering the room would make straight for the backbreaking seat.'

'Darling,' breathed Claire. 'That's brilliant. You must put it into *Shah-oh-Shah*. That's the title of the play Tiger's been working on. It's something absolutely new . . . '

Tiger nodded. 'Revolutionary.'

'Something he's never attempted before. In *Shah-oh-Shah* he actually uses dialogue.'

'Conversation,' interpreted Tiger.

Julia asked whether the play had anything to do with the troubles in Persia.

'Of course not,' Claire assured us, 'that would be so unsubtle, wouldn't it? Not Tiger's style at all.

'That's the one thing I have against Russia,' said Tiger. 'The Russians spend far too much on buying foreign agitators. We all know that they want to take over Africa. And no one can accuse Britain of not helping them. But the Russians should draw a line *somewhere*. Very well, Persian oil goes to South Africa and Russia wants to have a Communist government there. But why can't they leave it to Britain to mess up South Africa? Why must they inconvenience the Shah of Persia?'

'Darling,' the sadness in Claire's gold-speckled eyes was touching, 'all this is so nerve-wracking, but – whatever happens – you mustn't abandon the play. There are enough catastrophes in the world without depriving your audiences of *Shah-oh-Shah*.'

We'd obviously come to the heart of the matter, the misfortune our young son had mentioned. Had Tiger's imagination ground to a halt? Or was a more cosmic cause disrupting the creative process?

'It's no use.' Misery deepened Tiger's already low voice. 'If I needed proof that *Shah-oh-Shah* has been overtaken by real events, our stay at Balmoral left me in no doubt.'

'You mean *Balmoral?*' asked Julia.

'Yes . . . well the Royals ask us up occasionally. Seems we have a relaxing effect on H.M.'

'Last time was different,' said Claire morosely. 'Do tell them, darling. They've always been keen on your plays, so they're entitled to know what's stopping you from creating the new one.'

'I suppose it began when we built this house,' Tiger told us. 'The initial idea for the play . . . '

'It was the workmen. They opened Tiger's eyes,' Claire encouraged her husband. 'They did such extraordinary things.'

'Like spending hours of the working-day sunbathing and eating?' asked Julia.

'Precisely,' agreed Tiger.

'Who were your builders?'

'Cobbler & Sons Ltd.' said Tiger. 'Ernie and his mates were the men who gave me inspiration. In the end a Chinese firm . . . Mr Choy's cousin actually . . . completed the building. But I'm sure – well, almost – that it was our local men who gave me the insight into the society of the "eighties".'

'Especially into the new elite,' suggested Claire.

'Yes, the trade unions,' said Tiger. 'I had my revolutionary dramatic vision all worked out... and then *slam*, Balmoral, H.M.'s guest Sir Ivan Conniver. Newly knighted fellow, you know. Secretary of BAWLS...'

'We're hopeless at abbreviations,' Julia admitted.

'BAWLS is the *Building Artisans and Workers Labour Society*. Society, mark you, not trade union. You see the significance? BAWLS no longer needs industrial unity, because it *is* the industry. H.M. – as usual – was absolutely wonderful; the soul of consideration and tact. But even H.M. found Sir Ivan Conniver's pushfulness a bit tiresome. When I discovered what he *really* wanted I realized that my play was doomed . . . still-born. Just think of it! Overtaken by fact, miserable true fact!' Tiger gave his handkerchief to Claire. 'Darling, don't cry. Think of all the other disasters in the world . . .'

I asked him what Sir Ivan had wanted of H.M.

'It's too preposterous. He'd applied for a coat of arms for BAWLS . . . a bat and a hamster rampant, holding a hammer and sickle. And he had the nerve to ask H.M. whether BAWLS could put underneath the coat of arms *By Appointment to H.M.* Would you believe it!'

'Isn't that idea rather a good sign?' asked Julia.

'Well, it might mean that trade unions like BAWLS are moving away from Communism . . . becoming more sensible and all that. But this development's smashed up my whole play.'

In the sudden silence the greyhound bitch, which had been breathing down my neck, grabbed the Russian fish, and pulled it to the floor. As the dish was made of heat-resistant plastic, it didn't break.

Andromeda had devoured the best part of the fish when

our perfect hostess controlled her feelings about the still-born *Shah-oh-Shah*, picked up the fish and put it back on the table. 'Julia darling . . . Michael . . . Meda's left us quite a bit. Do help yourselves.'

The evening with the St George Clemenses had done us a lot of good. We wandered home, through the warm moon-lit country-side, feeling that we shouldn't kick against fate despite cracked chimneys and splintered floorboards, Ernie and his mates. Disasters happened in many forms, and perhaps many of them were non-disasters provided one didn't over-react.

Curate's Cottage was enveloped in a scent of roses, and we were savouring the fragrance of our country home when a tall shadowy figure came weaving towards us. Father-in-law.

'Had a good dinner?' he asked sourly.

'We were at the St George Clemenses.'

'Didn't they invite me?'

'You weren't around, daddy. We thought you'd gone back to London.'

'Said I'd see you through the building job . . . Had to make do with steak and kidney pie.'

'That's good at the Craftly Arms.' Julia put her arm through her father's.

'All right to go with a snifter. Not my idea of a dinner . . . got some bad news for you. Greyhound you've been playing around with. He's gone. Hopped it.'

Twelve

The Colonel told us that he'd been after Tango for the past three hours, searching grounds, fields and village. Judging by the over-enunciated account of his efforts I reckoned he'd spent most of the time at the pub. He didn't deny that he'd looked in for a snifter or two.

'Expected Tango to show up at the Craftly Arms,' he told us.

Julia, who'd been staring at the greyhound's empty bed, turned on him. 'I suppose Tango had a date with you.'

'No need to be sarcastic, girl. Thunderstorm, while you were dining and wining at Tiger's. Ask your husband . . . lots of animals dead scared of thunder and lightning. Need reassurance, don't you know . . . human company.'

'At a pub.'

'Girl's got a bad memory,' said the Colonel, pityingly. 'Just like her sainted mother. Michael, *you'll* remember that airedale who used to visit the pubs . . . name's slipped my mind.'

'Jock,' Julia told him, 'Sabina Webb's dog. Michael, we're wasting time . . . '

'Big, heavy dog,' her father recollected. 'Went to the Arms regularly, especially in bad weather. Told me yourself, didn't you? . . . Dog coming into the saloon, dripping wet. Everyone sorry for him . . . buying him half-pints.

Always stayed until closing time. Always up to the last customer to take him home. My opinion . . .'

'Based on a series of one case . . .'

The Colonel ignored Julia. 'Assumed the greyhound's the same psychological type as Jack.'

'Jock, daddy.'

'Jack. More confidence in people than in his own kind. Bit nervous of Streaky, isn't he? Nervous of bitches too . . . says Ernie. Put Tango in a trap next to a bitch and he loses the race every time. Must mean something.'

'Daddy, go to bed,' pleaded Julia. 'You're swaying like a straw in the wind.'

'See here, girl! Never yet fallen flat on my face. Won't put up with any nonsense from you. If you ask my opinion . . .'

'Michael . . .' Julia crowded me out of the shed. 'Where *could* Tango have gone?'

'Your father's probably right . . . not about the pub-crawling. Tango might have got scared of the thunder-storm and made for Ernie's place, wherever it is. Anyway, there's nothing we can do now. I'd better take your father upstairs.'

'Don't worry about him.'

'I'd rather he didn't break his neck.'

'He won't.' Julia watched the Colonel stalk into the cottage. 'It won't be the booze that'll get him in the end . . . it'll be the widow of Senator Pittsburgh, or another well-heeled dog-lover.'

We followed the Colonel. The crash I'd dreaded didn't happen, and presently the gurgling in the water-pipes proved that father-in-law was inexorably carrying out his nightly routine. According to Julia, he'd shaved last thing at night ever since her mother had died. The way he was, looking at it, wives had to take the rough with the smooth but other women might object to having stubble ground into their faces. And the Colonel, an incurable optimist, wasn't going to be caught out even when sleeping in his grandson's narrow bunk.

Wandering up to our bedroom Julia was smiling. 'What a parent!'

'We can take it. He's the only one we've got.'

'I wish we could phone Ernie.'

'Even if we had a telephone, I bet his number's not in the book. No use upsetting ourselves.'

'I'll change into jeans . . . '

'No point, love. Tango'll be safe. He's not stupid.'

At the risk of blowing the fuses I switched on the light. Suddenly Julia yelled like a Scot doing the sword dance and hurled herself at the top bunk.

Stretched on it, full length, head on pillow and Julia's night-dress tucked under his chin, lay the missing greyhound.

There couldn't be much wrong with a hound that had managed to vault through an open window, to negotiate the stairs and launch himself – with little take-off space – into the top bunk. A walk in the early morning confirmed my impression that Tango was fit for racing.

Before he'd hurt himself in that unscheduled chase after the rabbit his hind-quarters had moved as lithely as a calypso-dancer's hips. Now he was once again ready for speeding. Held back by the lead, his exuberance expressed itself in a comic wiggling of the rump.

At the boundary between garden and public footpath I let him off the lead and he went sailing over the flint wall. When I put him back on the lead he grabbed it in his teeth, arguing against the restraint, and it took some strength to convince him into a mere trot.

We skirted the sand-pit and took the track to the village. The moisture rising from the damp grass made the sun look like an orange on a Christmas tree. Church spire and pub, shrouded in the haze, appeared as ethereal as a mirage.

There was nothing ethereal about the twins, Mrs Glib and Miss Godley. Mrs Glib was picking up rubber bands, obviously discarded by the postman, and stuffing them into the pocket of her overalls. Miss Godley was putting a sandwich board outside her shop, which advertised a pop star newspaper and its reports on the latest industrial disputes.

'Strikes, I call it,' Miss Godley informed me. 'If I were the government I'd make the layabouts work a newsagents' single-handed . . . just for a couple of weeks.'

'Or a post office,' said Mrs Glib. 'You don't know what it's like, Mr Morton. The paperwork! You'd think them that's making the new rules and regulations are getting a productivity bonus for creating the bumf . . . Me and Mr Glib used to go to bingo in the old days. Now the evenings are gone. By the time we're finished with the paperwork there isn't even a TV programme worth watching. I mean, you get tired of the same faces, don't you?'

'Don't know about that,' Miss Godley pondered. 'I like to see the tops of the announcers. Keeps you up to date with what's being worn in London.'

'Mr Glib gets narked when he sees strikers or pickets on TV. That coat, he says to me as often as not, is worth eighty quid if it's a penny. If *they* can afford to wear clothes like that they don't need more wages.'

As I stepped into the gutter, by-passing the sisters, Miss Godley patted Tango's head. 'I didn't know you had a greyhound, Mr Morton.'

'He isn't mine.'

'Ah!' Miss Godley exchanged looks with Mrs Glib. 'It'll be Ernie's dog then . . . How's your building?'

'Getting on, slowly.'

'Mr Clive's studio's nearly finished.'

'Is it?' I tried not to show what I felt.

'No one can say that Ernie's not a hard worker, if he gets down to it,' said Miss Godley.

'He hasn't been knocking himself out at our place.'

'I dare say. But there's the long evenings and weekends . . . '

I let Tango pull me away.

'Oh, Mr Morton!' Miss Godley called after me. 'Will you tell your wife, I'm sorry the *Craftly Woman* will be late this week. It's a bumper issue . . . with stories about the Queen's lovely little dachshunds. The extra pages have made it that heavy, my boy's gone on a go-slow.'

At Simpkins's shop Tango and I turned into the twitten, a shortcut through the allotments to Clive Astley-Appledore's family home. As our architect's new studio had been started about the same time as the work on Curate's Cottage I wanted to compare the progress.

I hadn't expected that the timber from Shoreham would not only be stacked but almost used up. The cubist studio-structure stood gleaming in the sunlight, looking somewhat like a computer which had fallen off a space laboratory. Inside, the place was a hive of activity. The plumber, who'd deserted us, was soldering; Dicky was sawing away at a piece of wood, Ferret sweeping away piles of shavings. And Ernie was wielding a screwdriver. When he saw me and the dog his arms dropped to his side.

I looked at my watch. 'I was expecting you at Curate's Cottage.'

'Yeah.' He looked uncomfortable, but not for long. 'Me and me mates had a consultation about that. Me mates said as how it's against union rules . . . working alongside non-union labour.'

'What the hell are you talking about?'

'You. You're doing your own decorating, right? You're not a member of Allied Trades or something, are you?'

'None of your business.'

'That's what I mean, see. Could be a dispute situation, couldn't it?'

'If that's what you want you can have it.' I took the lead off Tango, chucked it at Ernie, and walked out.

Tango went bounding after me, but I ignored him. I didn't expect the fat boy to catch me up; yet he did, panting and puce in the face.

'Mr Morton, sir . . . ' The *sir* must have hurt him. 'Look 'ere, I didn't say I *was* in a dispute situation, now did I?'

'I don't care what you said. I'm busy.'

Ernie kept trotting beside me. 'Don't take on Mr Morton. I'll be round at your place at nine.'

'I'll get on faster without you.'

'Don't know 'bout that; you ain't got no tools. Right?'

True. I debated with myself whether to buy the most necessary tools or to borrow them from Tiger. What with building experimental stage-scenery he was bound to have *some*.

'How's Tango then?' Ernie sounded depressed.

'Ask his vet.'

'Mr Morton, Tango's been off the track too long. It's costing us money, me and me mates.'

'That's normal nowadays. The employer – that's you Ernie – always loses when there's a dispute situation.'

'You mean, like . . . I've employed you to look after Tango and . . . '

'You're quick on the uptake.'

'Mr Morton, we've got to consider the dog. Tango's taken a fancy to you.'

'So what.'

'Well, Tango's human, isn't he?'

'Don't insult your dog.'

'There you are. Admitted it yourself, and you a vet. Tango's a great dog. He *wants* to be fit again. It's 'is life, is racing. So you got to get him right . . . Or is he fit now?'

'Better ask his trainer.'

'He isn't going back there, see. We're switching Tango to kennels nearer Brighton, me and me mates.'

'So that's it.' Things began to fall into place. Tango had not been *home on holiday*, but waiting to be admitted to new kennels.

'Tango's booked in where the Duke of Edinburgh's taken 'is dogs, see.'

'Oh, I do. Those kennels mightn't be too keen on accepting a lame dog.' With Tango now beside me and the fat boy at my heels I marched on towards the High Street.

'Mr Morton, sir . . . me and me mates'll get your job done for you, and no mucking about. Honest. So long as you keep looking after Tango until he's okay.'

'Sorry, I'm on vacation.'

'But you're his vet. Like you said, I've been employing you.'

'And now we're in a dispute situation.'

'Me and me mates was only 'olding discussions, Mr Morton.'

'Please yourselves.'

'We'll leave Mr Clive's job and go ahead with yours.'

'I'm not interested in your promises.'

'Look 'ere, sir. You need builders, we need a vet. Right? If we don't get Tango back to racing soon we'll 'ave to pay for 'is keep out of regular earnings, see.'

The first day of the new *understanding* between Ernie and me induced in us a form of mild hysteria. It began when Julia, choking with laughter, fetched me from the garden and made me peer through the keyhole of the back door. Ernie was taking down the wall he'd begun to demolish with a sledge-hammer, but he'd drastically changed his method. Holding a chisel between the index finger and thumb of his left hand, a hammer in his right, he was delicately tapping away the mortar binding the bricks.

Lifting off a loose brick he handed it to Ferret, who brushed it and carefully laid it in a wheelbarrow.

I had to duck away fast or the men would have heard both of us laugh like maniacs. In the afternoon Julia felt sleepy, a symptom of emotional exhaustion, and retired to her bunk. I took Tango for a walk. On my return the men were still working steadily, most of the dividing wall was down, and I thought a word of appreciation would be good for labour-relations.

'Doing a nice job,' I said to Ernie.

'Yeah.' He executed four successive taps twice, then stopped and listened.

I heard the same taps, in exactly the same rhythm, repeated from somewhere above our heads.

'Funny.' Ernie looked distinctly uneasy. He went to work again, this time producing an uneven series of taps. The echo, which was unlike any echo I'd ever heard, followed. He handed me the hammer and chisel. 'You try.'

I did, choosing the beat of *I've got a lovely bunch of coconuts*. The answering tattoo gave me a good idea of what was happening.

'They say the cottage is haunted,' said Ernie. He pushed up his woolly hat and scratched under it.

'You don't believe that, do you?'

'Never know. Hundred years ago a curate who lived 'ere got the sack. They say it was an account of the vicar's wife . . . In them days you couldn't sue the boss for wrongful dismissal. So the curate went to Australia or somewhere like that . . . and got eaten by them cannibals. Verger's dad says 'e's been seen in this cottage since. Heard too.'

'Well, if there's a ghost he's a friendly one,' I assured Ernie.

'How's that then?'

'It's only friendly ghosts who manifest themselves in broad daylight.'

'Funny.'

'Ernie, you carry on with your work and I'll go and have a word with the . . . curate.'

'Dunno.' He looked uneasy and shamefaced.

'He'll stop his nonsense, I promise you.'

I left the kitchen and shot upstairs, knowing perfectly well what I'd find. My Julia must have had some talent when she was employed at the *Purple Pigeon*, The Top-Man's Top-To-Toe Show in Soho, before we were married. I heard Ernie's knocks below, saw Julia in a bikini and tap-dancing shoes on the landing, and pounced.

We hit the floorboards together and I stifled her giggles against my chest. 'Who told you about the wicked curate?'

'Mike.'

'Oh Lord!'

'The boys are thrilled that we've got a ghost.'

'There's not going to be any more haunting, love. You scared Ernie.'

'Good. Perhaps it'll stop him playing us up.'

'It'll stop him, more likely.'

'Oh no! Has he run away?'

'I promised him I'd make the curate behave himself . . . Listen.' Down below Ernie was tapping again, hesitantly at first, then with more confidence. 'We might have lost him for good . . . now, when he's at last putting his back into it.'

'It sounds wonderful,' Julia cocked her head, 'sort of syncopated.'

'You're not going to dance again,' I put Julia down and took off her shoes, 'not until our builders are out for good.'

Julia snatched the shoes out of my hands. 'I was enjoying myself.'

'What are we going to do with them?'

'The shoes?'

'Better not let Ernie see them.'

'I'll lock them up in my suitcase,' promised Julia.

Ernie's mates, apart from Ferret, didn't turn up, but Ernie himself lived up to his reputation of being a hard worker. The electric wiring was inspected and passed, the plumbing – though noisy – worked, and I was beginning to see how much the alterations were going to improve the cottage. While I got on with the painting and papering Julia scrubbed floors and cleaned windows with astonishing enjoyment.

One day we found Ernie, surrounded by tin-foil tubs, tucking into a Chinese lunch. Mr Choy's automats for drive-away dinners, *from receipes created by Buddhist Monkesses trained in the mysterious Eastend*, was open to the public. We decided to give up shopping and cooking and save time by living on Chop Suey and Eastend Chow Mein.

We were looking forward to seeing the last of Ernie, and Ernie was looking forward to delivering Tango to his new training kennels, when Tango suddenly began to behave oddly.

Even when the muscle in his thigh had been painful Tango had been keen on walking, impatient for the lattice-gate to be opened. But one morning, about a week after I'd considered him as fit as he'd ever be, the dog refused to leave his bed. Even Julia, with a piece of cheese, couldn't coax him out. The cheese – Tango's favourite food – remained untouched.

He was quiet, too quiet, while I examined him. I found no sign of pain or discomfort, nor did he have a temperature. Yet he seemed utterly dispirited, and every now and again he shivered. The most worrying thing was that he wouldn't touch any kind of food.

At midday he allowed Julia to pull him out of the shed, dutifully lifted a leg, and slunk back to his bed. We decided to leave Tango alone. By evening he'd surely be hungry. But in the evening he again turned away from everything we offered him, including Canadian cheddar.

That night we went to bed as miserable as if one of our boys had fallen ill. I had to admit to Julia that I had no idea what was the matter with the dog. And Julia assured me, with little conviction, that Tango must have *eaten something* and that he'd be his usual greedy self in the morning. I wanted to believe her, yet I knew instinctively that I was up against something outside my experience.

Thirteen

Whatever was ailing Tango couldn't be due to anything we had done, yet I was thankful that it had happened at the week-end when Ernie wouldn't be breathing down my neck. We felt desperate enough to let the Colonel have a go at persuading Tango into taking some nourishment.

As the three of us stood watching the dog in his bed, I went over the routine of the past days for the umpteenth time. The dog had eaten all we'd given him; his kennel was clean and airy; putting him on a long rope had allowed him a larger than usual run; Julia had groomed him meticulously; and between us we'd given him plenty of exercise.

'Dog's in a bad way,' said the Colonel. 'Put a can of beer in his dish. Didn't even sniff at it.'

Julia was too dispirited to tell her father that we didn't want Tango turned into an alcoholic. 'What about the cheese, daddy?'

'Wouldn't touch it.'

'Coming for a walk, old boy?' Father-in-law took the lead off the nail and jingled it. Tango turned his head away, but eventually allowed himself to be led out of the shed. It was a sad sight – the big animal slinking behind the Colonel, ears limp, tail tucked under.

In the evening the Colonel insisted that we should take

Tango to the Craftly Arms. 'Dog's used to crowds. Cheer him up.'

There was a certain logic in the argument, and we were at our wits' end. Tango didn't, as I'd hoped, leap into the car but he permitted Julia to put him in.

As usual on Sundays, the saloon was fairly full. Ernie and his mates weren't there, much to my relief, but Kath Greatorex and her brother were propping up the bar.

Kath, having exchanged her customary riding gear for a flowered dress, was looking quite handsome. 'Natterjacks are all organized,' she announced. 'Going to Whitney Dunes, thanks to Jasper.'

'Daddy?' Julia was dubious. 'What did you do?'

'Got hold of Bunny Grey, of course.'

'Bunny . . . ?'

'Girl's got a shocking memory,' the Colonel apologized for his daughter. 'Just like her sainted mother.'

'Daddy, do you mean the quartermaster who was in Ghazipur with you?'

'Who else? Obvious man for the job. Better than any vet I know. Secretary of . . . some society or other – name escapes me – organization for the protection of rare animals.'

'He's coming down next week,' Kath told us, 'prepared to stay on until he's found all the natterjacks. Isn't it good?'

'Splendid,' agreed the Colonel. 'Will ask Bunny to stay with us.'

'You won't,' said Julia, sharply. 'The cottage isn't ready for guests.'

'Mean *you're* not ready, Julia.'

'All right, I'm not.'

'Don't you worry,' soothed father-in-law, 'Bunny's used to roughing it. That time when our camp was flooded . . . '

'Daddy, *no*.'

The Colonel shook his head. 'Dear me. No sense of priorities – some females. You'd think frilly curtains were more important than special toads.'

'I'm not making *frilly* curtains,' Julia objected furiously, and illogically.

The Colonel ignored her. 'Same thing all through nature. Female of the species throws the spanner in the works . . . '

'What's that supposed to mean?' I hadn't seen Julia so angry in years. 'Better explain . . . since you're such an expert on females.'

'Stupid things males do, usually the females' influence . . . Take this poor dog,' the Colonel put a hand on Tango's head. 'Ever seen the likes of it? Remember the hunter I used to ride out in Ghazipur . . . most placid stallion I'd ever handled. No trouble at all until Nicky Bollinger bought a mare . . . quite a bit of Arab in her . . . '

'Daddy,' Julia dug her fingrs into her father's arm. 'Stop rambling . . . please. You were going to tell us something about Tango.'

'Who?'

'The greyhound. He's standing beside you. Remember?'

'What about him?'

'He's gone off his food.'

'Not surprised.'

'Why? Why, daddy?'

The Colonel turned back to Kath Greatorex. 'Telling you about Nicky Bollinger's mare, wasn't I? Funny thing was . . . '

I said, 'Let's hear about Tango first, Jasper.'

'Poor brute.'

'If you have any idea what's happened to Tango . . . '

'Nicky Bollinger's mare . . . '

Julia was holding on to herself gallantly. 'Daddy, you're supposed to care about dogs.'

'Best companion in the world, a good dog.'

'Spanner in the works,' prompted Julia. 'Remember?'

'Course I do, girl. Bitches . . . always did upset Rex . . . dog I had out in . . . '

'That's it,' murmured Julia. 'I think I know. Michael, let's go.'

'What about your father?'

'He can walk home.'

'After closing time?'

'There's Kath . . . there always is a Conny or a Kath.'

The Colonel, immersed in the story of Rex, didn't notice our departure. It was still light outside; blackbirds and thrushes, with a choir of sparrows, were giving their evening concert.

As we approached our cottage, Tango, with the amazing instinct of his kind, wakened up and acknowledged the nearness of his territory by pushing forward between the driver and passenger seats.

For the first time since his hungerstrike he began to *talk*, making those high-pitched noises in his throat. Suddenly we saw the cause of his excitement – a strange greyhound. It was standing, sniffing around the doorway of the shed – Tango's kennel. As I stopped the car it pricked up its ears, backed and went crashing through the shrubbery towards the vicarage.

Julia wanted us to watch Tango's quarters, all night if necessary. I was in favour of leaving the lattice-gate open and Tango on the long rope. I was almost certain that the intruding greyhound had been a bitch. No other explanation would have accounted for Tango's depression. We knew that our dog wasn't upsetting him, and we knew that his track performance had suffered whenever he'd been racing next to a bitch.

Why shouldn't there be dogs, I asked Julia, which were nervous of the opposite sex? Humans were, not infrequently. Nor was such behaviour unknown in other species.

'We can't leave Tango unprotected,' she said.

'Tango isn't a helpless little pup.'

'But if bitches scare him . . . '

'Why not give that one a chance to get to him?'

'She might reduce Tango to a nervous wreck.'

'He couldn't be in much worse shape than he is now.'

'Michael, I don't like it.'

'For all we know Tango might be frustrated rather than scared.'

'Look here, you did say that some creatures are nervous of the opposite sex.'

'Well, it doesn't mean that they're bound to remain nervous all their lives.'

In the end we left Tango as I had suggested.

Neither of us slept well that night. I heard Julia get up and go to the landing window facing the kennel. I myself got up twice. All remained quiet; no phantoms appeared in the moonlight, no sound came from the shed or its surrounds.

At daybreak I went down to see the dog. I was at the front door when a tawny bitch came wandering out of the shed. She looked about her, stretched, yawned, became aware of me and fled before I could get to her identity tag.

I emptied a large tin of dogfood into a bowl and took it to Tango. He fell to and didn't leave a scrap.

Not until Ernie and Ferret arrived did I realise the extent of my relief. Tango was about to go to his new kennels and Ernie wouldn't have taken kindly to a postponement due to an unidentified ailment. As it happened, I felt confident that another twenty-four hours of good feeding and exercise would restore the greyhound to prime condition.

My confidence was short-lived.

The last we'd seen of Tango had been at four-thirty when Ferret and Ernie had knocked off work. At six the dog had disappeared. The rope, still damp, was lying in the grass – gnawed through.

'Told you,' gloated father-in-law. 'Female of the species spells trouble.'

Julia smiled, 'Daddy, you should get your priorities right. What with your common-law wife in London and . . . '

'Don't you call Conny names, my girl. *Common-law* . . . vulgar, very vulgar. Sounds positively criminal.'

'In your case it probably is. As I was saying,' Julia mimicked her parent, 'Conny in London, Kath in Craftly . . . seems to me it's the male of the species that spells trouble *for himself*.'

'Rot. Tango'd still be here if it weren't for that fly-by-night bitch.'

'At least we know where to find him.'

We thought we knew.

Fourteen

The forecourt of 2001 looked like a market of second-hand clothes and furniture. On the gravel, in the centre of the jumble, lay a big Persian carpet and on it stood a group which included Mr Choy and his wife Rosie, bionic Inga and our sons. Thanks to our familiarity with Claire and Tiger's lifestyle we realised that the lumber hadn't been dragged out of doors because of a plumbing disaster indoors, but that Tiger was engaged in the experimental staging of his latest play.

Claire, scintillating with artistic fervour, put a finger to her lips. 'Tiger's started work on *Shah-oh-Shah* again,' she whispered, 'Isn't it super!'

'He's going to try it out in Craftly?' asked Julia.

'Yes . . . world-premiere here, in the autumn.'

'Mike and Andy will be away at school.'

'They're just standing in for Giles and Toby, Dave Thornton's boys. They're busy with the harvest.' The Siamese cat on Claire's shoulder swished its tail; it brushed Claire's elegant nose and made her sneeze. 'Chang-Ching's become so restless,' she sniffed. 'One would think she's on heat, not Andromeda. Meda's making an absolute fool of herself.'

'We know,' I told her. 'She's pursuing Tango.'

'The greyhound who's staying with you? So that's where she's been.'

'We're just trying to find him.'

'I wonder where Meda's got to.' Claire was obviously more concerned about the activities on stage than the disappearance of her bitch. 'Isn't Inga absolutely super!'

The big German girl, the slave-bangles on her ankles clashing together, was prostrating herself before Mr Choy.

The Chinese touched her with his toe, a fine gesture of disdain, which made Inga fall back in a spectacular double somersault. 'The womans of Persia abhorate you!' she yelled at him.

'Abhor,' corrected Tiger.

'She's playing an unliberated mother,' explained Claire. 'You don't think she's miscast, do you?'

'The womans are revolting,' Inga's accent thickened, 'and their childrens vill no more pimp the gasoline out of the grounds . . . '

'Pump.' Tiger made a note on his clip-board. 'Let's have *oil*, shall we?' He glanced at Claire. 'We'll change to *gasoline* when the play goes to the States, don't you think?'

'Super,' Claire agreed.

'The little childrens,' Inga continued, 'vill . . . '

'Mike's not that little,' objected our younger son.

'It's only theatre,' Mike pacified him. 'Come on Andy! Your turn . . . You're the trade union boss. You've got to tell the crowd all this stuff 'bout the Russian take-over . . . '

'Harken unto me,' declaimed Andy. 'I have come among you, the common herd . . . Mike, that's against the race-relations law.'

'Why?'

'Cause Inga's German and Mr Choy's Chinese, and it's rude to call them *common herd*, and . . . '

'Oh, don't stop,' urged Mike. 'We'll ask Tiger 'bout that after rehearsal.'

'I've come among you,' Andy picked up his lines, 'the common herd, with gifts of guns and caviar . . . Sorry; caviar-style lumpfish . . . '

'It's not really like the nativity,' whispered Claire, 'though it is three foreigners who're bringing the gifts. Do you think Andy's right about the race-relations law?'

'We'll think about it,' promised Julia. 'Right now we've got to find Tango.'

'Oh . . . well, if he's with Meda he'll be in the orchard. Meda absolutely adores the peacocks.'

The peacocks greeted us with those raucous cries that made Julia suspect them of being the souls of long dead sergeant-majors. We criss-crossed orchard and grounds without result. Though the perimeter of the St George Clemens's property was fenced with chickenwire there were spots which wouldn't have presented any obstacle for a roving greyhound or bitch.

When we got back to the house Inga and our boys had gone, the rehearsal finished. Rosie and Mr Choy, Claire and Tiger were having drinks at the kitchen table.

'You must taste our 2001 wine, darlings.' Claire poured a greyish liquid into a couple of down-to-earth beer mugs. 'It's the best Tiger's ever made.'

I asked where he was growing his vines.

'Wine made from grapes is out . . . absolutely finished,' he told us.

'Positively antique,' confirmed Claire. 'Tiger took a bottle of vintage claret – a bottle he'd bought at his wine merchants' – to Winkie's laboratory . . . '

'For analysis,' explained Tiger, 'super wine, mind you, but Winkie didn't find a trace of natural grape in it . . . What do you think of the 2001, Michael?'

I took a sip. The 2001 left behind an after-taste which reminded me of sour soil and mouldy cardboard. 'Unusual.'

'That's what everybody says.' Tiger was pleased. 'Amazing, isn't it? Trade secret, you know. The public's so hide-bound. People would accuse the wine-merchants of fraud if they knew that very few wines are made from grapes nowadays . . . unless one pays at least five hundred pounds a bottle at a Sotheby auction. Just proves how antique grape-wine is.'

'What is it ye've put in this drink?' asked Mr Choy, with professional interest.

'Actually it's dead easy. I buy packets of Claret-Type Quick-Mix at the supermarket. It comes out of the deep-freezer. Says on the label *made from the finest synthetics.* The instructions are inside.'

'Tiger adds extras, of course,' said Claire. 'I think it's the sodium glutamate which makes all the difference.'

'Isn't that dangerous?' asked Julia. 'I read somewhere that it can induce cancer.'

'Only if one eats large quantities of it,' Tiger assured her.

'Aye,' Mr Choy nodded, 'it's tasty stuff. We use a fair amount in our drive-away meals.'

'So that's what the *herbs* are.' Julia wrinkled her nose. 'We've been eating your drive-away dinners.'

'That's a shame.' Mr Choy looked upset. 'Ye're our neighbours. If we'd known we'd never have sold you yon rubbish.'

'It isn't rubbish,' objected Rosie. 'Lee takes a lot of trouble grinding up the vitamin pills that go into our drive-aways.'

'Aye, lassie. But I think Mr and Mrs Morton might favour the dishes we cook for ourselves. To this day my family won't touch yon chemicalized foods. My mother's cooking ruined my palate for convenience meals.'

'Fussy.' Rosie smiled, proudly. 'Lee'll eat nothing that's not made with fresh meat and veg. Even the eggs must be free-range.'

'It would cost you a wee bit extra,' said Mr Choy. 'But if you'd rather have drive-aways blended from the dishes we cook for ourselves, ye'd be welcome. Wouldn't they, Rosie?'

'That's right. It'll cost you twenty pence less if you bring your own containers.'

'More 2001?' offered Tiger.

Julia hastily moved her glass. 'We mustn't ... Tango ... '

'Wasn't it sweet of them,' Claire got up to see us out, 'they came specially to watch the rehearsal.'

'And to look for Tango,' I reminded her.

'Didn't you find Meda?' Claire glanced under the kitchen table.

'Neither Meda nor Tango. They must have jumped the fence and ... '

'Never ... Meda never jumps. She's much too lazy.'

'She managed to grab the Russian fish off your table,' said Julia.

'Now, let's be logical about this,' suggested Tiger. 'Domestic animals – like people – are creatures of habit. Claire, where does Meda normally go when she isn't busy killing the lawn?'

'The orchard. It's her love-hate relationship with the peacocks, and ... '

'We searched the orchard,' said Julia.

'Meda sleeps on your bed, Claire.' Tiger went to the door. 'Soon see.'

He was back so quickly that I missed the last chance of pouring my 2001 down the sink. 'Not on the bed ... Let's keep calm. There must be a rational explanation ... '

'Oh Tiger!' wailed Claire. 'You're so right, darling. I should have remembered. Oh my God!'

Fifteen

The destruction Meda and Tango had wrought in Tiger's study hadn't been as fatal as the disaster of the birth-giving cat Claire had remembered with so much alarm. The cat had borne her kittens on the graph-paper on which Tiger had drawn his wordless play *Psht*, and the amniotic fluid had disintegrated the lines.

The two greyhounds had just played among the typed sheets, which Tiger normally scattered on the floor – probably for the pleasure of seeing Claire reverently pick them up. We'd managed to collect the crumpled pages – all but two, which Tiger might have mislaid – and put *Shah-on-Shah* together again.

What had compensated Claire and Tiger for the mishap to the typescript was the satisfaction that their bitch had mated with a *suitable* dog. One couldn't control the amorous adventures of cats, Claire had told us, but if one didn't control a pedigree bitch one richly deserved mongrel pups. So, wasn't it absolutely fabulous that Meda herself had been so fastidious in choosing the father of her off-spring? To think that she might have taken a fancy to the Thorntons' labrador-collie mixture or that shaggy horror at the Craftly Arms.

Tango, none the worse for his escapade, had slept longer than usual and spent the following day eating his head off. At four-thirty Ernie at last took him away to deliver him to his new kennels, and we saw him go with mixed feelings. We wouldn't have to spend so much time on walking the greyhound; on the other hand Ernie might well lose interest in completing our building work. He'd finished the structural changes and even patched up the crack in the living room chimney, but the kitchen units were still lying in the hall and the floor hadn't yet been renewed. If Julia had contented herself with a vinyl cover I myself could have put it down, but she'd insisted on octagonal quarry tiles, in character with the cottage. I reckoned that even Ernie would lay those tiles better than I.

After Tango's departure we didn't expect Ernie and mate to show up. But they kept coming at eight-thirty and worked on fitting the kitchen units four hours out of eight – not a bad record.

We were beginning to savour the promise of completion when Julia discovered the flaws. Where the wall had been removed between the old kitchen and scullery the supporting beam was set too low so that the ceiling was already beginning to sag. The new sink-taps were dribbling. We found a number of holes in the walls, which hadn't been made good, and there was daylight showing between a new window-frame and an outside wall.

'Let's face it,' Julia was studying the lumps of cement which formed a ragged ridge on the floor where the old wall had been imperfectly removed. 'Ernie's made a lousy job of it.'

'These bits and pieces can be put right,' I comforted her.

'The floor will never be even unless he chips off the old cement before he lays the quarry tiles. And he won't do it.'

'Then I will.'

'Michael, the point is, you shouldn't have to do these things. What are we paying for?'

'Whatever's in Clive's specifications.'

'That's a joke. *All work will be carried out by craftsmen*, etc. etc.,' quoted Julia, 'and *completed* etcetera. Why can't these miserable botchers finish one job before they smash into the next?'

'Maybe Ernie's a Muslim at heart. Muslim craftsmen – the ones who built those amazing honeycomb ceilings in mosques – used to leave one part unfinished. They wouldn't make anything perfect for fear of offending Allah. The idea was that Allah alone is perfect.'

Julia laughed. 'For God's sake don't tell Ernie . . . The real answer is that Ernie's not only a lazy con-man but a slut. Don't look so surprised; there are far more male than female sluts in the world. Thing is . . . how are we going to get all the defects put right?'

'I don't know, but we'd better say nothing until Ernie *thinks* he's finished.'

'Don't leave it too late. Once Ernie's gone we'll never get a man from Cobblers' back on the job.'

'Let's play it by ear.'

The mystery of Ernie and mate turning up daily, despite the fact that I was no longer taking care of Tango, was explained on the Thursday after the hound had gone to the kennels.

Ernie, resting in the garden, a fat cigar stuck in his face, a can of beer at his side, was watching me cut up the branch of a sycamore. 'Mr Morton.'

'Yes?' I stopped sawing and wiped the sweat off my face.

'Tango's racing tonight. Brighton, seven-forty-five.'

'Going to watch him?'

'Yeah. You coming?'

'No.'

'Want to see 'is form, don't you?'

'Not particularly.'

'You should, seeing as you're 'is vet. Vets should know about greyhound racing.'

'I do know, but I don't go in for it.'

'Missing something, aren't you?'

'Don't think so. I've got other things to do.'

'Not tonight, you 'aven't. You got to see Tango run... on account of it's the first time since 'e hurt heself. Me and me mates got to be sure Tango's 'undred per cent like.'

'You'll know by his performance tonight.'

'Me and me mates reckon *you'll* know better . . . Don't you want them quarry tiles laid nice and even, and none cracked? They was 'ard to get, them tiles.'

'What's that got to do with Tango?'

'I'm 'uman, aren't I? Never can get them kind of tiles laid proper like when I got something on me mind.'

'You won't have anything on your mind by tomorrow.'

'Depends, don't it? If Tango don't run well, I'll 'ave something on me mind all right. And if 'e does run well I'll be worried like, in case it was a one-off show . . . Tell you what; I'll pick you up at six-thirty. You can take Mrs Morton. We don't mind.'

We drew the line at going to Brighton in Ernie's car, but go we did – not because blackmail had become our way of life, but because I hoped I'd be better able to manage Ernie if I kept track of him and Tango. Julia on the other hand was eager to see Tango again. She'd become attached to the big brindled hound with his aware eyes and his amiable temperament.

I was in no doubt that Ernie was pleased we'd come. He and Ferret, Dicky and Mr Cobbler, placed their first bets at the Tote and then insisted on buying us drinks.

The atmosphere of the Stadium seemed to me more frenetic than at horse-racing. There was more noise; people moved around at greater speed, and the bookies were positively besieged by punters with fistfuls of crumpled ten-pound notes. The scurrying was presumably due to the organization peculiar to dog-racing, eight races per evening, each race lasting a mere thirty seconds. Perhaps it was a fallacy, but I had the impression that between those swift races and the sixteen or seventeen-minute intervals one could lose one's shirt much more easily than on a race course.

We didn't bet on the first race but bought a few twenty-pence Tote-tickets for the second because Julia liked the name of one dog – Andy of Pickleswith. Andy, first to shoot out of the traps after the electric hare, was a relatively small black dog with desperate determination. He almost fell at a bend but recovered sufficiently to come in second.

Before the fourth race Ernie assured us that he had a hot tip, told us to back Egremont, and handed a hundred pounds or more to a bookie. We didn't back Egremont, but Julia was quite excited over Ernie's big stake. How could he afford it? she asked me. Didn't she know by now? I asked her.

Egremont did run well though it looked at the last moment as if he'd been beaten. It turned out a photo-finish with Egremont a half-nose ahead. Ernie and his mate had trebled their money. They celebrated with drinks all round and gave up betting until the last but one event – Tango's race.

'Putting your shirt on 'im, Mr Morton?' asked Ernie.

'No, it's the Tote for us.'

'Tote for me too, seeing as it's 'is first race after 'is trouble.'

Tango went after the hare at a respectable pace, but I had the impression that he wasn't going full out by any means. Long, easy strides. Enjoying himself. No trouble with the hip. Just not trying. He came in third all the same – not too far behind the winner.

Surprisingly Ernie was beaming with pride. 'Seen the way 'e took the bends? No dog like 'im. Outrun the lot if 'e put 'is mind to it.'

'Pity he didn't put his mind to it,' said Mr Cobbler, flatly. 'I'd say that's why they put long odds on him.'

'They wouldn't 'ave put long odds on 'im in Doncaster or Wolverhampton.'

'You can't get away from it, Ernie. No concentration . . . that's always been Tango's trouble.'

'Not 'is fault. Trainer's fault. That's why we've changed kennels. Right?'

'I don't know.' Mr Cobbler was unconvinced. 'I doubt that they'll ever cure him of going haywire when he's running against a bitch.'

'Tango's the greatest. But if you don't fancy 'im no more, guv'nor, me and me mates'll find somebody to buy you out . . . like Mr Morton 'ere.'

Tango was undoubtedly fit, I had outlived my usefulness as his vet and yet – amazingly – Ernie did turn up the following morning. We'd been unable to discover his special skills – if he was in fact any kind of craftsman – until we saw him go to work on those octagonal quarry tiles. Not only was he laying them with impeccable precision, he was obviously enjoying it.

Father-in-law, who'd also been watching Ernie, beckoned me into the living-room, where Julia was putting up curtains.

'Fellow knows the job,' he observed.

'Yes, if he finishes it we'll have a good floor in the kitchen.'

'He'll do it. Fact, he'll finish all the jobs in the house if I have anything to do with it.'

Julia turned. 'Don't interfere, daddy. Please.'

'Wouldn't have got where you are if I hadn't . . . interfered. Fellow doesn't need you any more, Michael. Not clear why he's bothered to turn up at all.'

'Perhaps he has a passion for laying octagonal tiles,' suggested Julia.

'Rubbish. Mark my word.'

Ernie and Ferret took the shortest ever lunch-break – half an hour. The sight of the fat slob putting his heart and soul into a real job of work was so extraordinary that I kept popping into the kitchen. At four-thirty-two he was tapping yet another tile into place.

'Working overtime?' I asked him.

He looked up at me, making me regret the joke. 'Wasn't thinking.' He rose from the floor, nimble despite his bulk, and began to strip off his overalls. 'Got Tango on me mind.'

'You were pleased with his performance, weren't you?'

'Yeah . . . Don't like the guv'nor's attitude though.'

'Well, he'd have liked to see Tango win.'

'Don't see as 'ow Tango *can* win.'

'Come on, Ernie . . . that isn't what you thought last night.'

'Dog can't win if 'is owners don't believe in 'im.'

Did Ernie mean that? Was he superstitious enough to believe that Tango's performance could be influenced by Mr Cobbler's lack of faith? It seemed incredible, and yet I was convinced – in retrospect – that Ernie had been genuinely scared by the tapping of the *curate's ghost*. Or *was* it so incredible? More august people than this crafty countryman had been known to believe in the spirit world, including a distinguished air-marshal. And hadn't Shakespeare said something about *more things 'twixt heaven and earth*? Something told me that it would be a mistake to laugh at Ernie's assumption.

'Tango's racing again next Thursday. You wouldn't . . .'

'I would not.' My sympathy evaporated. 'You can't have been serious . . . suggesting that I should buy Mr Cobbler's share in Tango.'

The Colonel had come in and was listening with interest.

'It's good sport,' said Ernie, with little conviction.

'I'm not keen on spectator sports.'

'Didn't think you was . . . but it's different if it's your own dog racing, see.'

'Forget it.'

'Butters!' The Colonel's crisp voice made Ernie stand up straight. 'What's all this about? Selling a share in that greyhound of yours?'

'We'd like to, sir . . . me and me mates.'

'Might consider it.'

Ernie's mouth fell open. 'You sir?'

'Prepared to consider it . . . Now, don't stand about, man. Off you go.'

When Ernie and Ferret had left I went for father-in-law. 'You shouldn't have done that. He wants somebody to buy Cobbler's share in Tango, and he's serious about it.'

'So am I,' asserted the Colonel.

'What do you know about greyhound racing?'

'Used to go to the dogs before you were born. Real sport in those days. Lots of doping going on, not like nowadays.'

'All the same, buying yourself into a syndicate isn't something you should do on impulse.'

'Not exactly an impulsive sort of chap.'

'I didn't think you were until . . . '

'Thinking of Conny . . . '

'As a change from Kath?'

'None of that, boy! Conny happens to be the lady I live with. Owe a lot to her . . . '

'Such as the trip to India you've been promising her.'

'Damned expensive nowadays.'

'Yes,' I'd picked up the Colonel's wavelength. 'Giving her a share in Tango would be much cheaper. You might get away with it.'

'Mad about dogs, isn't she?'

'Dog-breeding. That's not the same thing.'

'New experience for her . . . same as the Indian trip.'

'Well, Tango might do her for a while.'

'Year or two. Might go to tracks all over the country.'

'That's not as cheap as you think.'

'Cheaper than air-tickets to India . . . and the type of hotels Americans like.'

'Jasper, do you know how much it costs nowadays to keep a greyhound in training kennels? And the cost of transport to the tracks?'

'Share the costs. Member of a syndicate.'

'You seem to have made up your mind.'

'Certainly not. First, want to see dog on the track.'

'You shouldn't have raised Ernie's hopes.'

'Can't handle people . . . that's the trouble with your generation. No problem, Butters. Leave him to me.'

Sixteen

The Colonel, according to his daughter, had never shown any talent for creating happy personal relationships. His wife had stuck with him because it would have been complicated to escape from somewhere in the middle of Asia, because she'd had nowhere else to go, and because she'd been vaguely interested in Julia. Mrs Hanley hadn't been downright unhappy with her husband; he had, at least, provided her with servants which – in turn – had given her the time for sublimating her dislike of him by painting pictures of savage tigers and snakes.

The Colonel's relationships after his wife's death, from an unspecified fever, had never achieved permanence. Julia put it down to the fact that his romantic impulses were so short-lived that even the dimmest women soon tumbled to the monumental selfishness behind dear Jasper's charm.

That his relationship with Constance Pittsburgh had lasted so long was no doubt due to the fact that Conny's selfishness and thickness of hide matched the Colonel's and that she was wealthy enough to consider a replacement for him if he no longer pleased her.

Julia and her father had remained in touch because it had suited him to have a second home and because Julia hadn't succeeded in ridding herself of the belief – instilled in her by her father – that children owed a duty to their parents.

As to the Colonel's male acquaintances, Bunny and Ronny, Nicky and Jimmy had usually complied with the Colonel's requests for the sake of an unshakable faith in the old-boy network, and possibly as a gesture to the nostalgic memories of the vanished Empire and regimental high jinks in remote corners of the world.

I was sure of one thing; I'd never yet met a man who did father-in-law a favour because he liked the Colonel. Yet Julia had sometimes accused me of having a sneaking regard for her preposterous father.

The nearest I'd ever come to approving of certain qualities in the Colonel's character was in the last days of our building operations. Even Julia had to admit that there was something formidable in the way he stood over Ernie and Ferret from the moment they arrived at our place until they left at four-thirty.

Ernie was eager to see *his* tiled floor finished, the Colonel determined to have everything else completed first.

The moment Ernie would tip-toe into the kitchen and get down to the floor I'd hear the Colonel's voice trumpet, 'Butters! Where are you, man?'

Julia pleaded with her father. 'You'll drive him away, just when we most need him. It really does take a craftsman to lay the tiles.'

'It'll be done,' promised the Colonel, with undiminished arrogance. 'Females! Why must they always interfere? Better go and get some decent steak. Michael and I are tired of the Chinese rubbish you keep pulling out of the slot-machines.'

'Daddy, no one's asking you to stay.'

'Fine mess you'd be in if I didn't.'

There was an understanding between father-in-law and

Ernie that the Colonel would go to Brighton on Thursday, see Tango run and then give his decision whether or not he'd buy himself into the greyhound syndicate. Without putting it into words the Colonel had made it clear that the deal would not be unconnected with the completion of the work at Curate's Cottage.

As late as Thursday midday the damaged floorboard in the living-room hadn't been replaced, the holes around the pipes under the sink hadn't been filled in, nor had the worrying gap between the kitchen ceiling and its supporting beam.

'Butters!' roared the Colonel. 'Leave the damned tiling alone. Come here!'

Ernie lumbered into the living-room. 'Yeah?'

'Got to get this board down. Don't want my daughter to break a leg.'

'Board's got to be cut to size,' grumbled Ernie.

'Then cut it, man. And mind you cut it straight.'

With Ferret's help Ernie spent an hour fitting the board.

'Colour doesn't match,' the Colonel told them. 'Got to do something about it.'

'Need some stain, see.'

'Haven't got it?'

'No.'

'Slapdash organization . . . Where can I get the stuff?'

'Simpkins's.'

'Very well. While I get the stain you'd better fill the gap between the ceiling and the beam. Should have done it properly in the first place . . . Michael, watch how he does it. He'd better put in oak-wedges. Use the floorboard he damaged. Good old stuff . . . won't shrink.'

When the Colonel hadn't returned within the hour I assumed that he'd dropped in for a snifter or two at the Craftly Arms. However, he did show up an hour and a half later – with a can.

'Butters!' he yelled.

Ernie, who'd gone back to his beloved tiling, jumped.

'What about the living-room, Butters?'

Ernie shrugged his massive shoulders.

'Haven't yet finished in there.'

'Didn't 'ave the stain, did I?'

'Here,' the Colonel thrust the can into Ernie's hand, 'get on with it.'

'Little job *you* could be doing instead of . . . '

'Beg your pardon, Butters? Say something?'

'No.'

'Glad to hear it. Get your skates on, man. You haven't got all day.'

'Never get them tiles down now.'

'Browned off, are you, Butters?'

'I'm only 'uman.'

'Just what I was thinking. Greatest thing about human beings . . . infinite capacity for fighting against odds . . . winning through.'

'Yeah?'

'Certainly.'

'Not if you're made to stop what you're doing all the time.'

'Shouldn't have left so many jobs unfinished, Butters.'

'Kitchen floor won't get finished, that's for sure . . . not by four-thirty it won't.'

The Colonel watched as Ernie finished staining the new floorboard. It wasn't looking too bad.

Ernie straightened up. 'Can I get back to me tiles now?'

'You can start again.' The Colonel took a paper from his pocket, Julia's list of botched and poodle-faked jobs. 'I'll make a tour of inspection, Butters. If you have attended – properly, mind you – to all these items, I'll let you carry on.'

'Won't get all them tiles down, not by four-thirty.'

'Don't see what's so special about four-thirty.'

'You know . . . '

'Not that I'm aware of.'

'It's when we knock off.'

'No law against – er – knocking off at five or six, is there?'

'Look 'ere . . . '

'Beg your pardon?'

'Sir. We're going down to Brighton tonight.'

'I'm acquainted with your intentions.'

'We got to go 'ome and 'ave our tea.'

'Eating too much, obviously. Look at yourself, man. Bad for your heart, carrying all this surplus weight. Drop down dead, one of these days. Shouldn't be surprised.'

'Yeah? . . . Well, we got to get changed, see.'

'Why?'

'We can't go in our work-gear, now can we?'

'Don't see why not. Not ashamed of holding down a job, are you? Anyone care what you're wearing?'

'Me wife.'

'Rubbish. Man doesn't dress up for his wife.'

'There's some as got respect for marriage.'

For the first time in his dealings with Ernie the Colonel looked somewhat uncomfortable. 'Don't stand around, man! Or none of us will be going to the dogs tonight.'

Ernie worked on the floor without a pause until the last tile was in place. At five-fifteen he ripped off his overalls, gathered up Ferret and his tools, muttered at me *this'll cost you extra*, and sped away in a storm of flying gravel.

Julia and I were so shaken by the sudden ending of our building agonies that we sank into the garden chairs and remained bereft of words until father-in-law joined us with tumblers and a bottle of scotch. I felt as weary as if I'd delivered a byreful of cows.

'Drink up, you two,' said the Colonel. 'Snifter'll do you good.'

We obediently drank.

'Going to have a bath,' announced father-in-law, 'before Julia hogs all the hot water. Better get ready.'

'All right, daddy, let's go out for a meal. We could try the Manor Restaurant at Nether Craftly.'

'Michael, what's she talking about?' The Colonel made it sound as if Julia had broken into fluent Bulgarian.

I said, 'A special dinner. We've earned it.'

'Nonsense. Dinner can wait. Going to Brighton . . . all of us.'

'Daddy, I really don't feel up to . . . '

'Strong young female, aren't you? Do you the world of good . . . change of scene . . . bit of a flutter . . . Tango.'

The mention of Tango did it. 'Well,' said Julia, 'maybe . . . '

'Sandwiches and beer at the races. Nothing wrong with that.'

'Daddy, you don't like sandwiches.'

'Can't have it soft all the time. Got to get one's priorities right.' The Colonel took something from his hip-pocket . . . my cheque book. 'Michael, you owe me five hundred quid. Want your cheque now.'

'What!'

'Good God! Feckless lot, you youngsters. Never occurred to you that this thing had to be organised in advance, did it? Just as well I took it in hand.' He put a wad of ten-pound notes on the table. 'Here you are. Five hundred in cash. No need to count it.'

'What's it for?'

'Bit slow, aren't you? Warned Julia when she got engaged to you . . . Got to have cash on you tonight. Going to have a flutter, aren't we?'

Seventeen

Shirt-pockets aren't made for carrying fat wallets, and five hundred pounds in notes make a bulky package. I was going to leave the money under my mattress. Julia said that no one was forcing me to gamble a penny but that it would be a pity to limit ourselves to twenty pence Tote tickets. I argued that there was quite a gap between five hundred pounds and twenty pence tickets; so why not take fifty pounds and leave the rest at home? She put it to me that burglars, statistically speaking, were more successful than pick-pockets and that the money would be safer on my person.

In the end she borrowed her father's blazer, which had a roomy inside pocket, and persuaded me to wear it. Did I care that the blazer came down to my knees? That the sleeves covered my hands? Or that – despite the jacket hanging loose – I looked pigeon-chested? I did, until I noticed that half the men at Brighton Stadium had padded chests or behinds, and until I got caught up in the hornet-nest buzzing around the bookies.

Only once before in my life had I carried more than fifty pounds in my wallet – on the one occasion when I'd put a hundred pounds on a certain peer's horse at Ascot. I'd kidded myself that I knew the animal, but I'd lost what had then seemed a fortune and I'd never again supported the bookies.

I feared that Julia, in a state of euphoria after the completion of the building, would want to put real money on every race; but, like her unpredictable father, she contented herself with the Tote. Sweating in the woollen blazer, I placed no bets on the first three races. I couldn't be bothered to shoulder a way through the scurrying mass of punters.

Ernie, Ferret and Dicky lost on the first couple of races but made a few pounds on the third. Mr Cobbler hadn't turned up, which proved to Ernie that he really had *gone off* Tango. Ernie was depressed about it.

'He isn't going to win,' he told us. 'Stands to reason.'

'Not betting?' asked the Colonel.

'Dunno.'

'Got to back your own dog. Show a bit of spunk.'

'Money down the drain,' moaned Ernie.

The punters appeared to agree with him. At the end of the fourth race the odds on Tango lengthened. Tango was in the fifth race. Mixing with the crowd I heard a man advise his girl friend against backing him because he'd drawn the outside trap – which he disliked – and because he'd be running alongside Queeny – a bitch.

'Hear that?' the Colonel asked me.

'Doesn't sound good for the syndicate.'

'Rubbish. Buck up, Michael. Why d'you think I got you five hundred quid? Had a feeling this would happen.'

'Tango's prospects don't excite me.'

'No imagination, that's your trouble.'

'I can imagine losing five hundred pounds and I'm not keen on the idea.'

'Come on, man!' The Colonel crowded me towards a bookie who'd just changed Tango's odds from ten to twelve to one. He took out his snakeskin wallet and handed over a fistful of notes, around a hundred pounds. 'Put on the lot, Michael,' he pestered me. 'Haven't got all night. Race will be over in five minutes.'

'That'll be a relief.' I was expecting Julia to back me up. Instead, her eyes were luminous with excitement.

'Please, darling,' she urged, 'we do know Tango . . . '

'Good reason for not . . . '

'Just this once . . . put on the lot . . . please.'

While the bookie was counting my money I had the weirdest sensation that someone else had gone mad. Not me. No responsible family man with two lots of school fees to pay, and a hefty builders' bill on the way, would even consider a five hundred pound flutter on a greyhound – let alone a dog known to be mixed up about bitches.

'Good chap.' Father-in-law's voice seemed far away.

'Hurry up, Michael!' Julia went slipping through the crowd. 'Don't want to miss the race.'

'I'd rather have a drink.'

'Oh, darling! Don't be difficult.' She grabbed my hand and pulled me back to our place with Ernie and his mates.

'Well Butters?' asked the Colonel. 'Taken my advice?'

Ernie shrugged. 'Tote.'

'You'll regret it.'

I said, 'It's us who'll regret.'

'Nonsense.' The Colonel watched the dogs being fed into the traps. 'Matter of personal experience. Not mad about females. Never was. Trouble is . . . hooked once, done for. Could never again do without them. Tango's problem too, poor beast.'

Out on the track the electric hare was on the move. The traps flipped open and the hounds shot out like rockets. Golden Boy, on the inside, looked the best of the bunch, a powerful animal which went into the lead within the first few seconds. Queeny, the dark bitch next to Tango, promised to make second place. Though quite a bit smaller than the dogs she appeared to be blessed with flying feet. I didn't even look at Tango until Julia began to shout his name and the people around us joined in.

Something strange was happening. Golden Boy had just rounded the bend when his speed dropped dramatically. If he had hurt himself it wasn't obvious, yet he certainly appeared to be out of the running. Queeny turned her head, seemed to realise that she was in the lead and put on an extra spurt.

It was then, with the distance between Queeny and the rest of the runners lengthening, that I heard a high-pitched yelp. I couldn't be sure but it sounded like Tango's voice. At the same time Tango threw himself forward with an incredible burst of energy. In what seemed a split second he and the bitch were flying along neck to neck. Then Tango, turning inward, looked bent on stopping Queeny by belting across her path. I was expecting the race to end in disaster, with Tango as well as Queeny injured, when the Colonel deafened me with a roar of triumph.

Tango and the bitch had finished, Tango clearly in front of Queeny. The two of them were trotting along, way past the finishing line, Queeny looking over her shoulder, Tango barking at the kennel maid who was trying to prevent his mounting the bitch.

The Colonel thumped my back. 'Well, what did I tell you!'

Julia was hugging her father and me, Ernie watching us warily.

'Won a lot, 'ave you,' he asked.

'Can say that again,' crowed the Colonel.

'How much?'

I kicked father-in-law's shin, but he paid no attention.

'Few thousand between us,' he told all and sundry.

'Daddy!' protested Julia.

Too late. Ernie had heard. His dark, sullen eyes were upon me. 'Great. You'll need the money for paying them extras.'

'Extras?' asked the Colonel.

'Yeah, you 'eard. Put in a lot of work at Curate's Cottage.'

'That's what Cobblers' pay you for,' father-in-law told him. 'What with your tea-breaks and your botching they'll probably lose money on the job . . . poor sods.'

'Not if we charge the extras.'

'Such as?'

'Well, there's all them bits and pieces you made me do again.'

'Shouldn't have made a mess of them in the first place. Don't be stupid, man. Want me to buy Mr Cobbler's share in Tango or not?'

'Well . . . yeah, I do.'

'Ernie,' Ferret plucked at his mate's sleeve. 'Listen, we don't need '*im*. Tango's won. Right? We wouldn't 'ave no trouble finding another buyer. Me own brother . . . '

'Belt up.' Ernie shoved the little man aside. 'Don't want nobody like the guv'nor what don't properly believe in Tango, see. Colonel 'ere put a wad on 'im. Right?' He turned to father-in-law. 'You buying then?'

'Yes, if you stop trying to pull a fast one on my family. No extras.'

'Okay . . . no extras. But no vet bill from 'im either.'

'Done.' Father-in-law shook hands with the fat boy.

'Mind you,' Ernie looked thoughtful, 'you wasn't nice to me when I worked for you lot . . . not really *nice*. There's hostility money.'

'What!'

'Union got it for me mates what's on dumping waste, see. Reckon *we* could be entitled to hostility money.'

'Jump in the river.'

'Now don't take on, sir . . . Don't get me wrong. Didn't ask Mr Morton for hostility money, now did I? If me Union says so, the guv'nor's got to pay up, see.'

THE END

Wyndham Books are obtainable from many booksellers and newsagents. If you have any difficulty please send purchase price plus postage on the scale below to:

Wyndham Cash Sales:
P O Box 11,
Falmouth,
Cornwall.

or

Star Book Service:
G P O Box 29,
Douglas,
Isle of Man,
British Isles.

While every effort is made to keep prices low, it is sometimes necessary to increase prices at short notice. Wyndham Books reserve the right to show new retail prices on covers which may differ from those advertised in the text or elsewhere.

Postage and Packing Rate

UK

22p for the first book plus 10p per copy for each additional book ordered to a maximum charge of 82p.

BFPO and Eire

22p for the first book, plus 10p per copy for the next 6 books and thereafter 4p per book.

Overseas

30p for the first book and 10p per copy for each additional book.

These charges are subject to Post Office charge fluctuations.